A SERIES OF
LIGHT

manuscripts

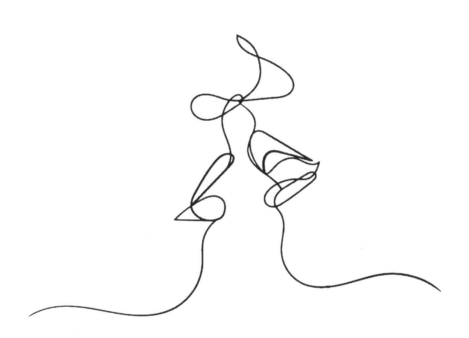

GAGE OXLEY

First paperback edition August 2020

ISBN: 979-8-6717-2624-4 (paperback)

Published by Oxygen

for a scribbled out name
that my love keeps writing
again and again and again and again and again

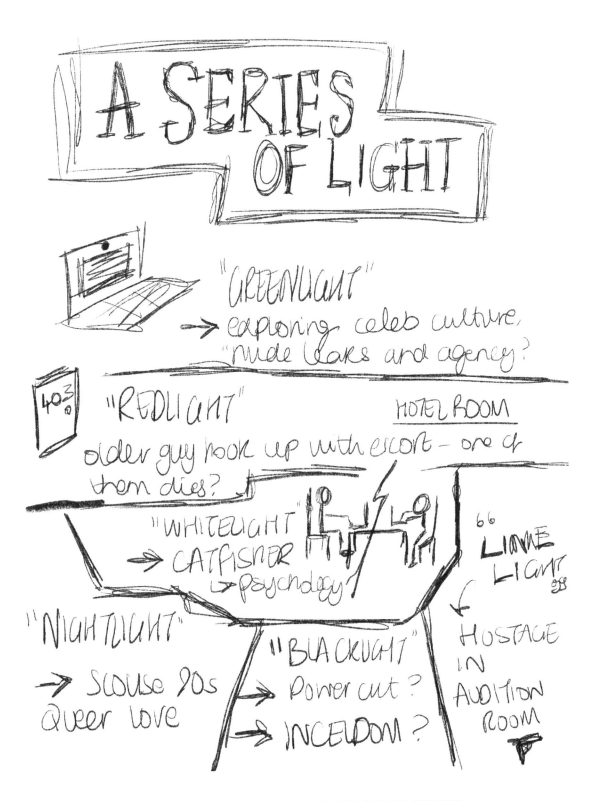

A SERIES OF LIGHT

"GREENLIGHT"
→ exploring celeb culture, "nude leaks and agency?

"REDLIGHT"   HOTEL ROOM
older guy hook up with escort — one of them dies?

"WHITELIGHT"
→ CATFISHER
  ↳ Psychology

"NIGHTLIGHT"
→ Scouse 90s
  Queer love

"BLACKLIGHT"
→ Power cut?
→ INCELDOM?

"LIMELIGHT"
HOSTAGE IN AUDITION ROOM

AN ORIGINAL CONCEPT MAP FOR THE SERIES [GAGE OXLEY]

CONTENTS

PREFACE

I wrote A SERIES OF LIGHT across a period of four months, starting October 2019 with "Greenlight", and ending in January 2020 with "Limelight". Though, I always stick to the rule that a film isn't finished being written until after an audience has seen it.

My intention with the anthology show was to present new themes, new ideas and new challenges which would inspire growth as independent creators. The majority of the storylines take place in a handful of rooms, usually with only one or two actors for our audience to meet. However, as I wrote the next episodes while on the production of the ones prior, inevitably I ended up becoming more ambitious and those rules swiftly became quite non-existent. Still, I feel the tone of the narratives we present as being one of claustrophobia, intensity and isolation.

A SERIES OF LIGHT provides a new exploration of queer narratives, one that I didn't have the chance to experience while growing up. These narratives are not explicitly queer in the same vein as popular LGBTQ* mainstream films, yet the representations are clear: gay people can be the villain, they can be in love, they can be totally confident in who they are, or they could be trying to figure that out. Queer voices are not something to be used as a side-character or sub-plot, and equally they should not be relegated to the stringent World of 'the gay best friend' or the throwaway token character to ensure 'diversity'.

I am proud of the narratives explored in A SERIES OF LIGHT's first season. They are provocative, tense, dark and light in places. We meet escorts, actors, catfishers and incels; experience love (and heartbreak) in the 90s as well as the modern-day trappings of a life online. When we made the show, I feel it's important to highlight that it presented me with some of my favourite "on-set" experiences. Produced by some of my closest friends, whose average age was 21, on next to nothing - what we all achieved against seemingly all odds is what I really cherish about this experience.

And so, I wrote and assembled this exploration of the series that means so much to me, in dedication to the hard working volunteers, and best friends, I could wish to have in my life. I hope you find inspiration through this as I did, and know that if you are reading this right now, it is you who inspires me to continue creating what we do.

With love, as always.

SAM

→ lost Soul
→ Manipulated
→ controlled
→ Romantic

GREENLIGHT
Written: 15 September 2019, Produced: 7 October 2019

Written by Gage Oxley
Story by Jack Parr and Gage Oxley

Jack Parr as SAM
Alexandra Marlin as CHLOE

INT. SAM'S BEDROOM - NIGHT
A quick hit into a darkened room, an extreme wide reveals the huge ceilings and ornate decor. And, a young guy, SAM, illuminated by a computer screen sat on a desk chair. He's totally stripped, breathing heavy, he splutters a moment as his arm shakes. As we track closer, but still at an extreme wide we see a wetness to his torso. He breathes heavy still, but calming. He clears his throat, stands up and walks away.

We slowly track in on the seat he was sat on as we hear moments later the sound of water hitting the shower floor. As we snake around his chair, stained with recent liquid, we turn to the computer. On it's desktop displays a paused video above which the logo for 'PORNTUBE'. But, our focus is on the circle above it, built into the desktop, for a second, the green light flicks on, and then off.

TITLE CARD: GREENLIGHT

We hear a dull vibration in the room, persistent - a ringtone. The shower stops as we track back out, and pan across the room to where Sam moved off to - the door opens and he steps out, towel around his waist. He hears the vibration and leaps to the phone on the bedside table. He swipes and answers.

SAM
Hey Chloe.

Chloe, on the other end, answers, and after a moment-

SAM
Have they sent the sides over? I can probably look over them after tomorrow's audition.

Sam unplugs the phone and moves over to the chair. He picks up a pair of boxers on the way and puts them on, a freshly ironed shirt on a hanger is pulled off and wraps around him as his phone is on his shoulder. We follow, as he sits, feeling the wetness of the arm of the chair. He brings it up, brows furrowing as he realises what's happened. He gets a tissue and wipes it off.

SAM
Okay, I'll look over them tonight then. Listen, did you hear back from Marv?

We slide round his shoulder and he clicks off of the porn, typing his name in and allowing an actors profile to come up - a busy page with an image of himself, looking slightly airbrushed and a bit younger.

SAM
Yeah, no, I really liked it. It's good. Moving on out of the child star phase.

On the screen, a push notification comes in "1 NEW EMAIL | Subject: I saw u...." Sam's eyes narrow, as his gaze moves to the notification. The cursor roams over the notification and click. We now see the email; as it comes up, Sam's eyes scan the page hurriedly. He moves the cursor along the text as he reads, so do we: "By opening this email you have started a timer. It is simple. You send us £10,000 or the world sees all of you. Just think of your fans, Mr Cooke! The attachment is just the start...."

SAM
Just let me know when you know more, Chloe.

Sam gulps, trying to stay calm. He clicks on the attachment and the screen is taken over by a grainy webcam screenshot of Sam, flushed red.

SAM
Shit.

Sam is horrified, his stomach in knots.

SAM
No, sorry Chloe. I'm... uh... can I call you back?

He doesn't wait to hear her answer.

SAM
FUCK!

Sam's hands fly to his head. A ping, another alert through in his inbox. "You have 5 minutes. I know you've seen the email. Did you enjoy ur shower? ;)" He looks at the webcam on his computer. He scrabbles around, picking up a blob of blue-tack and sticking it over the hole, but it's already too late.

SAM
Eva, start timer for 5 minutes.

There's a 'ding-ding' as his phone illuminates and starts a timer, 4:59, 4:58... He stands up, paces, where does he go from here?

SAM
FUCK! FUCKING SHITTING FUCKING CUNT!

He spits, furious. Then, he hurries back over to the chair; quickly typing in and then clicking, we hear a dial tone.

SAM
Fucking answer.

Then, a click as a young woman stumbles a bit as she holds her phone up.

CHLOE
Hey, you. Why you video calling me all shirtless? Please tell me you've got something on your bottom half.

SAM
Chloe I need you to transfer me ten thousand from my payment account and you can't ask me why.

He breathes out, heavily.

CHLOE
Sam, what's up? Is everything okay?

Chloe moves around, into a quieter corner.

SAM
Please just do this.

CHLOE
I... can't not ask why, Sam.

Sam bites his lower lip and looks around the room, eyes zooming around - hoping to seek an answer.

SAM
I got an email.

Chloe nods, waiting-

CHLOE
And...?

SAM
They want ten grand.

CHLOE
Who's they? Sam? What the fuck's going on?

SAM
They hacked my webcam. Okay? Please. I just need 10k it's not a lot.

Chloe clears her throat,

CHLOE
Okay. Sam, I get these emails all the time, it's a scam it's just-

SAM
It's not a scam. Chloe this could ruin me, my career. It's my money. I need it now.

Chloe pauses a minute, thinking.

CHLOE
This... this is going to sound crazy.

She smiles,

CHLOE
It could be great for you. For your image, I mean. You said it yourself you're tired of the squeaky-clean child star roles.

SAM
Chloe-

CHLOE
Hold on, this... if we manage this right we can get a front cover on Flare, Pose, every newspaper and website.

SAM
I'm not-

CHLOE
Throw in the whole "invasion of privacy" thing, get a hashtag going. You'll be up for loads of roles.

SAM
You're not listening.

CHLOE
And, trust me, I've seen it - you've got nothing to be ashamed about.

Sam snaps-

SAM
For fuck's sake Chloe, it was gay porn. I was wanking to fucking guys.

Chloe is left silent.

CHLOE
Oh.

Sam rubs his face with his hands, and ruffles his hair.

SAM
Yeah. So.

There's a beat, neither know quite what to say.

SAM
So I'm gonna need that money. Now.

He looks down at the timer, 2:24, 2:23.

CHLOE
Sure. Of course.

She's cold, sharper and quieter. She plants the phone down and drags open a laptop, quickly typing. There is a moment of silence as Sam watches. He leans forward, cradling his forehead in his hands.

SAM
I'm sorry, Chloe.

CHLOE
It's fine.

Sam looks up, Chloe is typing.

SAM
No, no it isn't. You know, it was job after job after job. Then I got the blue tick, then the screaming girls and letters. I could not put that at risk.

CHLOE
Mm-hmm.

Sam shakes his head.

SAM
You can't do this to me now, Chloe. You know what it would do to me, they say the industry's better but I'd be on my fucking arse! The career I've built, all the fans, the roles I want - it changes all of it.

Chloe snaps,

10

GREENLIGHT

CHLOE
Yeah and what about us, Sam? You don't think it changes me and you? Fuck's sake.

She types again, we see Sam - he looks over at the desk: a holiday photo, him kissing a smiling Chloe.

CHLOE
But no, it's always your career isn't it.

She stops typing. Sam looks, he can't say anything. He looks at the timer again: 1:02, 1:01.

SAM
Please. No, of course I care about you.

Chloe looks out across her room, thinking. Then, she shuts the lid. She moves over to the phone.

CHLOE
Just in case it isn't clear Sam, I don't hate you because you're gay. I hate you because you're a fucking arsehole.

The screen goes off, as Sam is left looking at his reflection. He sits back in his chair, empty. He can't do anything.

Song: Theme from "A SUMMER PLACE"

We slowly track in on him, lost, alone and isolated. Then, the chirping of an alarm. Sam doesn't even move, as it continues on and on, we get closer and closer to Sam. We hear the ping of a notification which stirs Sam from his trance.

He leans forward- clicking on a link, the page takes a moment to load, as it stutters we first see the headline: "CHILD STAR TURNED HEART-THROB SAM COOKE LEAKED!" Sam's eyes tear up-

SAM
Fuck.

He is startled by the phone on his desk, ringing - we track in on the 'unknown number'. Then to Sam, he looks down at the phone, staring - then up at the screen in front of him, tear-filled eyes almost shaking with fury.

CREDITS ROLL
END FILM

11

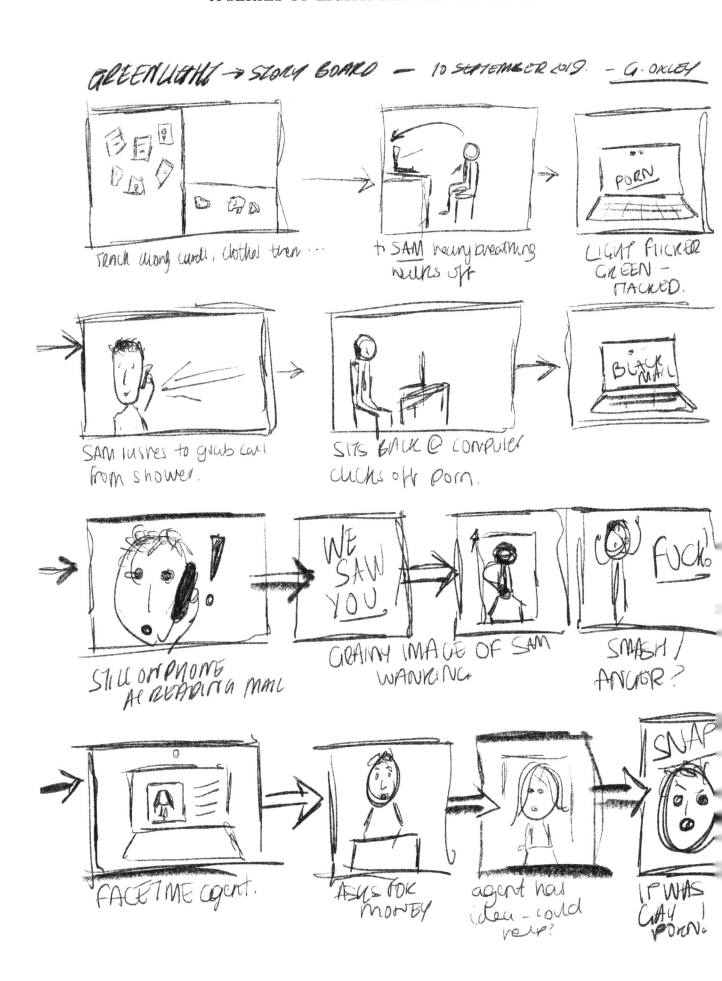

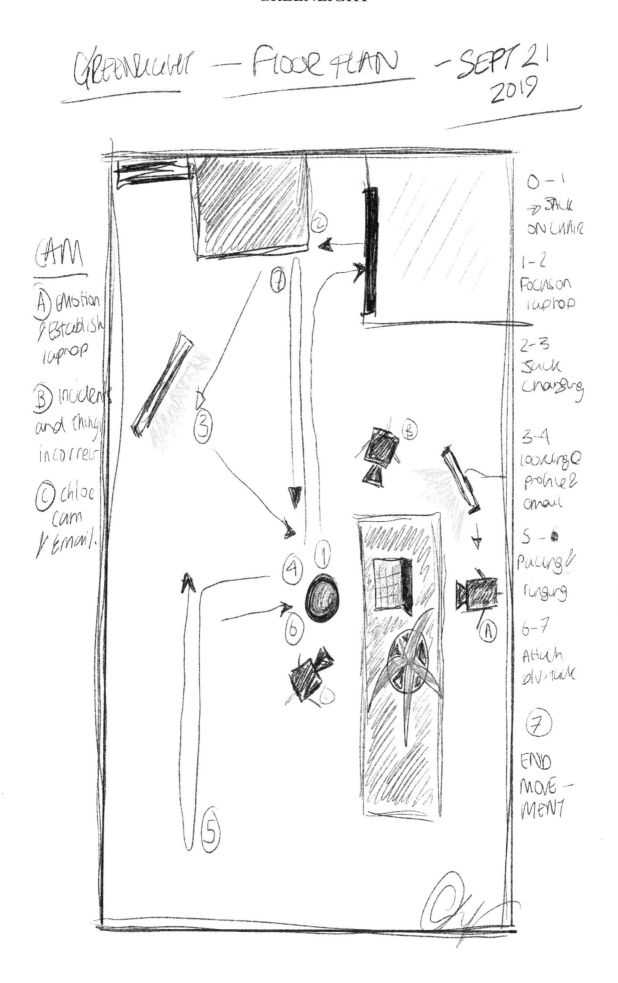

REDLIGHT
Written: 17 September 2019, Produced: 4 November 2019

Written by Gage Oxley

Jake Watkins as CALLUM
Dan Sheppard as JIMMY
with Thomas J. Harkness, Tiarnan Meely Clark and Gage Oxley as COLLEAGUES

1. INT. HOTEL ROOM - AFTERNOON
Open on a man, 56-year-old JIMMY, sat on a double bed of his hotel room, he's tightening his tie in the mirror. There's a knock at the door, and a soft voice muffled through the wall.

CALLUM (O.S.)
Room service.

Jimmy looks up, and a moment later stands and opens the door. A young man, dressed in bellboy attire, stands in the doorway - 17-year-old CALLUM.

CALLUM
Room service, sir.

He speaks softly, unable to engage eye contact. Jimmy, a taller and generally bigger man stands above Callum staring.

JIMMY
Well, come on in.

Callum squeezes through the door, he looks around the room - as if seeing it for the first time.

CALLUM
So we provide a complimentary-

He turns and as soon as he does Jimmy is on him, kissing him roughly. Callum is shocked, but freezes. Jimmy pulls away.

JIMMY
Complimentary, huh? Don't worry. I'll give you a big tip.

He laughs and launches on him again, kissing him hurriedly. This time, Callum breaks away.

CALLUM
I need to get ready, first. Can I use your bathroom.

JIMMY
Sure. But you got my message?

CALLUM
I know we need to be quick.

JIMMY
Colleagues will start wondering where I am. And - just to check - how old are you?

CALLUM
I'm seventeen.

JIMMY
Christ. I miss being that age.

He chuckles, now loosening his tie. Callum smiles and moves away into the bathroom.

2. INT. HOTEL ROOM - BATHROOM - CONTINUOUS
Callum walks in and shuts the door. He exhales slowly and quietly. He stares at himself in the mirror, tilting his head, observing himself he draws a line with his finger down his jawline.

He looks down and stretches out the crotch of his trousers. He snaps a pill from his pocket and quickly places it in his mouth, swallowing it down. He stretches his crotch again, and slips a hand into his trousers - adjusting himself. He spots a razor beside the sink and picks it up. He shouts through-

CALLUM
Do you want me to shave?

And then to himself-

CALLUM
Bet you'd like that. Fucking perv.

He puts the razor back down and stretches out. One final look in the mirror before going to leave.

3. INT. HOTEL ROOM - MOMENTS LATER
The door to the bathroom opens and Callum tentatively steps out. Jimmy is stood by the window, on the phone, mid-way through conversation.

JIMMY
- okay love.

Callum steps forward, unsure of what to do.

JIMMY
- well, Jess, daddy will be coming home tomorrow and we can go through it then. Ok. I miss you too. Is mummy there?

He turns round, hearing Callum behind him. Jimmy looks at him, rolling his eyes at the phone. Callum smiles. Then, slowly unbuttons his shirt. Jimmy's smile falters, looking at Callum.

JIMMY
Yeah - I'll have to schmooze the suppliers tonight, but the conference is nearly over.

Callum's shirt falls open. Jimmy stares, we're tight in on him as he eats every detail. Callum's hand slink down his torso onto his trousers and he starts unbuttoning slowly from the top.

JIMMY
Well of course Kevin's being a tosser. It's in his blood to irritate.

Callum drops his trousers slowly, stepping out of them, edging closer towards Jimmy.

JIMMY
Listen, darling, something's come up.

Callum is right in front of Jimmy now, staring up at him. He places his hand over Jimmy's free one and brings it over to the front of his underwear.

JIMMY
I'll speak later, okay? Love you.

Callum looks up at Jimmy and smirks.

CALLUM (whispering)
Love you too.

Jimmy quickly hangs up the phone, and Callum slinks away.

JIMMY
You shouldn't do that.

CALLUM
You shouldn't be doing this. Looks like we're both a little naughty.

Jimmy hurriedly unbuttons his shirt, pulling his tie off messily. It's hungry and desperate as he drags off his blazer.

JIMMY
I have 10 minutes.

CALLUM
10? Wow, okay. Are you sure you're going to be able to last that long?

Jimmy gives Callum a glare as he shoves his trousers down.

CALLUM
What's she called?

JIMMY
Huh?

CALLUM
Your wife.

JIMMY
Don't do that.

CALLUM
Is she pretty?

Callum moves over to the bed and kneels onto it.

JIMMY
Callum.

CALLUM
Does she go on top or do you fuck her like this?

Callum drops his back and throws himself onto fours. He laughs and turns over.

CALLUM
You're so tightly wound aren't you.

Jimmy finishes folding his clothes up on the chair beside the bed.

CALLUM
Why don't you loosen up?

Callum leans over and takes a small transparent bag with white powder from the bedside table and brings it up to Jimmy.

JIMMY
Are you serious?

CALLUM
Come on. Live a little.

Jimmy considers a moment, before sighing and nodding. Callum expertly taps the powder on the bedside table and hands a rolled up note to Jimmy who promptly kneels down and snorts. He hands the roll to Callum, who stands up, above Jimmy now - he pulls Jimmy up and places him on the bed. Now, Callum kneels and places the note to his nose. We see the powder disappear. Callum sighs, sniffing in. He turns and looks at Jimmy and smirks.

CALLUM
I'm going to give you the best 10 minutes of your life.

Callum moves towards Jimmy, his head lowering off camera, bobbing. We track in on Jimmy, a bead of sweat drips down his face as-
-we hard cut into Callum, on top of Jimmy, moaning as he rises and falls. His hands are placed on Jimmy's chest, balancing him.

JIMMY
I'm gonna-

Callum hurries his pace as Jimmy's breath hitches, a guttural splutter as he finishes - Callum softly exhales too as he slows. Jimmy clears his throat, coughing. He's spluttering, face turning even more red and sweaty. Callum slows to a stop but Jimmy keeps coughing, harshly now with more force.

CALLUM
Do you want some water?

Callum slides off of Jimmy who grabs his chest, as if something is stuck. At the side of the bed, Callum hitches up his boxers and grabs a glass. Jimmy barks now, saliva dripping from his lips. Callum runs back in and passes the glass over to Jimmy who struggles to bring it to his lips and drops it, splashing everywhere.

CALLUM
Fuck.

A hard splutter and bile seeps from Jimmy's mouth, and then, his neck loses it's tension as it tilts and a stream of blood creeps out of his nose.

CALLUM
Oh my god. Fuck. What the-

Callum looks around at the room, strewn bedsheets wrapped around the now dead Jimmy.

CALLUM
Shit.

He looks around, running to the phone and picking it up from its cradle. He presses three buttons hurriedly - a brief pause - before,

EMERGENCY SERVICES (O.S.)
999, what emergency service do you require?

He's about to answer before he stops- looking at the tablets on the side-table. Callum slams the phone down and grabs the tablets, he hurries into the bathroom.

4. INT. HOTEL ROOM - BATHROOM - CONTINUOUS

He throws the tablets into the toilet and looks around for something, anything. He catches himself in the mirror - pale, scared. Then, a knock on the door and he spins around.

COLLEAGUE 1 (O.S.)
Jim it's Kev. Shall we make a move?

Callum backs away into the bathroom. He doesn't know what to do, panic setting in. Another knock.

COLLEAGUE 1 (O.S.)
Jim? You there?

Callum brings his hand up to his mouth, buffering his breaths. Then a moment later we hear murmuring and footsteps away. Callum edges his way out of the bathroom quietly.

5. INT. HOTEL ROOM - CONTINUOUS

On tip-toes, Callum leaves the bathroom and into the main space. He brings his hands up to his head, shakey fingers threading through his hair. He steps in and we see again - Jimmy, coiled in strewn bedsheets, laid on the bed with a dark blood dribbled across his face from his nostrils.

Callum drags up the shirt from beside the bed and throws it on, as he does so he looks around the room - and stops at the body. Realising. Another wave of dread washes over his face. Callum sneaks closer to the bed, desperate to be nowhere near the body. He kneels on the side of the bed, lifting up the bedsheet, and with the other hand moving in. Moments later, he brings out a condom. He holds it loosely by the top, face reeking of disgust.

Then, a vibration. Callum spins around - seeking the cause of the noise. He sees, on the table beside Jimmy's folded clothes - his phone. Callum moves over, "KEV" is ringing.

CALLUM
Shit.

He looks up at the door, he knows he is running out of time. Still holding the condom tentatively, he scans the room searching for a place to dispose it. He eyes the bin - no - the kettle - no - and then, the window clouded by curtains. He hurries over to the window and opens it up. A moment of thought before chucking it out of the window.

CALLUM
Holy fuck.

Callum is desperate - he needs to get out. He rushes over to a carry-all bag beside the window, Callum scurries through the contents of clothes and papers. Then - bingo - he brings out a leather wallet, thick with notes. Callum's face lights up, shocked at the vast amount of notes stuffed haphazardly in the wallet. He looks over at Jimmy. Then, takes the wedge of notes. He pauses a moment and counts out - 10 - 20 - 30 - 40 - 50 - 60 - 70. He places the rest back in the wallet and drops it in the bag. He moves over to the side of the bed and picks up his trousers, sliding into them and tucking his open shirt into them. Another knock on the door.

COLLEAGUE 2 (O.S.)
Jimmy are you okay?

Another voice. And a louder knock.

COLLEAGUE 1 (O.S.)
I've tried ringing him.

There's more murmuring.

COLLEAGUE 2 (O.S.)
We need to go now.

COLLEAGUE 1 (O.S.)
Shall we ring reception?

Another knock on the door. Louder.

COLLEAGUE 2 (O.S.)
Jimmy. Jimmy - you need to open the door, can you hear us?

Then, one solitary hit on the door - louder, a shoulder? Callum steps back, terrified. He looks down at the body of Jimmy on the bed again. He's thinking. Then, he moves against the wall, towards the door. Another bang, and Callum slips into:

6. INT. HOTEL ROOM - BATHROOM - CONTINUOUS
He has an idea. He breathes out, hands shaking. He picks up a spare razor blade from the side of the sink. Thinking. He looks at himself one final time - how so much has changed. Another big bang on the door.

COLLEAGUE 2 (O.S.)
Shall we call 999?

Quietly, Callum slinks back out-

7. INT. HOTEL ROOM - CONTINUOUS
- and closer to the body on the bed. He looks at him and we see in greater detail now, arms, veins, the glossy eyes. Another bang, louder and crunchier. He needs to move quick. He looks down. Breathing out, terrified, white as a sheet as he sinks the razor into Jimmy's forearm. He slides it down, as blood quickly flows from the deep wound in his wrists. Callum breathes heavily, blood across his hands. He looks at the other side - he leans across the body, again atop him, as he replicates it on the other side - blood spraying across Callum's delicate and shaking hands.

A louder hit on the door and it crunches. Callum spins around. Has he been caught? No - but he needs to move - he races back into the bathroom.

8. INT. HOTEL ROOM - BATHROOM
He drags his bloody hands below his eyes, wiping the tears. He looks down at his hands, blood everywhere. What the fuck has he done? BANG - a huge noise as the door to the hotel room opens. Through the crack in the bathroom door, Callum watches two people move past - as soon as they do, Callum sees his chance and sneaks out of the bathroom.

9. INT. HOTEL ROOM - CONTINUOUS
In the foreground, the bodies of two men in suits who are frozen.

COLLEAGUE 1
Fuck me. What the fuck. Jesus Christ.

In the background, Callum sneaks out - into the corridor.

10. INT. HOTEL CORRIDOR - CONTINUOUS
Callum walks down the corridor, a smudge of blood on his face and covering his hands, shirt open. His face is torn with emotion. He breathes out, he's escaped. Someone races past him, a worker at the hotel who carries on down the corridor. In the background she reaches the doorway and we see her hands go up to her face.
As Callum walks, further and further, we slowly fade darker and darker until we reach black.

CREDITS ROLL
END FILM

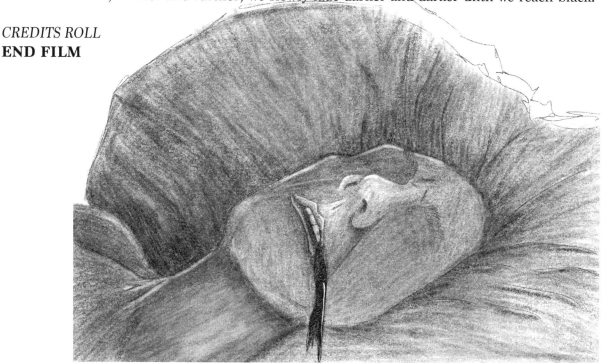

21

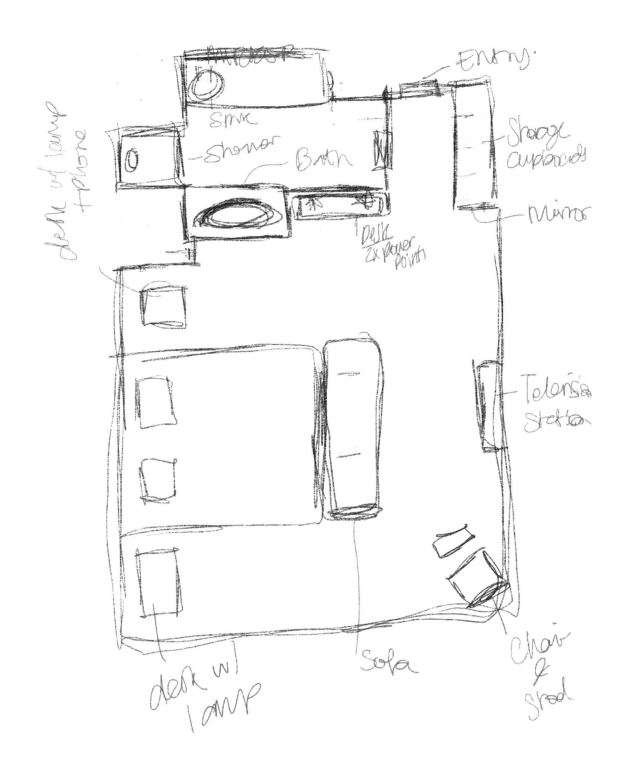

A ROUGH SKETCH OF THE FLOOR PLAN FOR THE HOTEL ROOM THE PRODUCTION TEAM SHOT IN. THE HOTEL ROOM WAS ORIGINALLY A LOT SMALLER, BUT THE HOTEL UPGRADED THE CREW A WEEK BEFORE, WHICH ULTIMATELY CHANGED A LOT OF DIRECTOR OF PHOTOGRAPHY, ROSE McLAUGHLIN'S SHOT IDEAS.

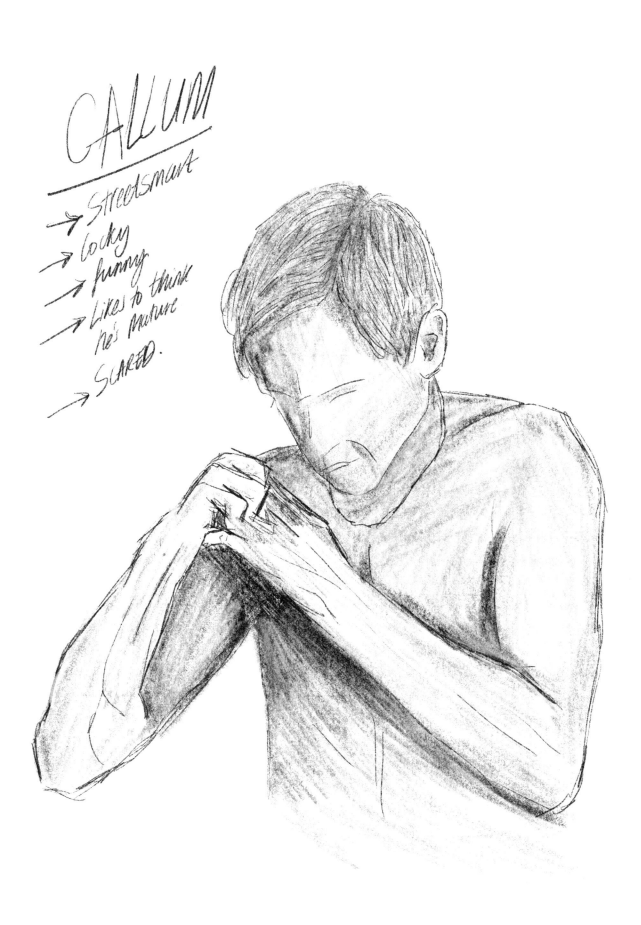

WHITELIGHT

Written: 14 November 2019, Produced: 23 - 24 November 2019

Written by Gage Oxley

Ole Madden as ARRON
Rochelle Naylor as AUBREY
Samuel Curry as MITCH
with Poppy Potts as CASSIE

1. INT. AUBREY'S APARTMENT - NIGHT

Aubrey, a 21-year-old woman sits at the computer, her legs up and crossed on the desk, leaning back in the seat. She is eating out of a tub of ice cream. We hear the 'plink' of a message come in. She smiles and leans forward - as the text comes up, we hear the voice of the sender.

MITCH (V.O.)
I'm not that surprised, I know you now Aubrey. The type who cuddles up with blankets and a book on a Saturday night rather than a nightclub.

She laughs, and types back-

AUBREY (V.O.)
You obviously don't know me. No blankets in sight. It's far too hot for that.

She leans back and waits, another scoop of ice cream. Then, *plink-*

MITCH (V.O.)
Oh really? Maybe you're wearing too much.

There's a winking emoji at the end of the text. Aubrey places the ice cream on the desk.

AUBREY
Fucking finally.

She pushes her hair back behind her shoulders and leans forward. She types back-

AUBREY (V.O.)
You think? What should I take off?

She bites her nails, waiting. We see the familiar drift of three bubbles, he's typing. Then, it disappears.

AUBREY
Come on.

Plink-

MITCH (V.O.)
Hmm. How about those cute little shorts of yours?

She opens a folder on her computer, and drags a photo across into the chat. Her, with shorts midway down.

AUBREY (V.O.)
Like this?

Aubrey in real life unbuttons her jeans' top button,

AUBREY
Now you.

AUBREY (V.O.)
How about you show me what boxers you're wearing tonight?

Aubrey releases the next button, and her hand slinks in when plink. We see MITCH, a twenty-something year old jock-type, traditionally attractive, in his boxers.

AUBREY
Oh shit.

Aubrey smiles, hand further in, when - we hear a door unlocking, Aubrey jumps and spins around to the sound of the door. The camera quickpans with it and at the door, as it opens, we see Aubrey stumbling in. As she does she looks up, hazy and drunk.

AUBREY
Were you wanking?

A cut back to an over-the-shoulder of the Aubrey by the door reveals a new person on the computer, 19-year-old ARRON who's hand is in his jeans, other hand shutting down windows on the computer furiously. His hand comes out and he pulls his shirt down to cover it up.

ARRON
No, no of course. How was your night?

Aubrey slumps in, crashing onto the sofa. She slurs-

AUBREY
It was so fucking good, Arron. We all missed you babe.

She snorts in, absolutely no inhibitions.

AUBREY
How. How did I get home?

Arron stands up, buttoning his jeans back up as he does so, moving over to Aubrey on the sofa.

ARRON
Listen, why don't we get you into bed?

Ping -

Arron looks up, at the computer, and back to Aubrey - she is laid eyes shut. He moves back to the computer and opens the window back up.

MITCH (V.O.)
You still there sexy?

ARRON
Shit.

He looks around at Aubrey. And types,

AUBREY (V.O.)
Yes. Baby you look so great in those Calvin's.

He sighs,

ARRON
Fuck's sake.

He hovers over the 'close' button when *ping.*

MITCH (V.O.)
How about we make these photos live? Maybe I could show you even more.
Arron shuts his eyes, then, drags the cursor away from the red close button.

AUBREY (V.O.)
Sure. Give me a min?

Arron puts his hands to his face, unsure of what to do. He looks around, Aubrey now laid flat on the sofa - breathing heavily - she's out. Then, a moment, a thought. He looks over at Aubrey again. He grabs his phone and moves over to Aubrey. Then, he holds his phone close to the side of her face. A flash, then, he moves. He races back over to the computer and drops his phone on a circular base. Then, a box pops up - he quickly drags content over from the folder to the chat. *Ping* - Arron opens the window again,

MITCH (V.O.)
Here's another one while you get ready.

And then, a photo comes through - Mitch's torso. Arron exhales. The transfer finishes, the photo he took of Aubrey definitely passes. He presses 'send'.

Then, the excruciating wait. 'Message Seen', another pause, then the writing bubble. Another pause. Then, the green dot beside Mitch's name disappears and is replaced with 'OFFLINE'. Arron scans the page, desperately. He rubs his eyes and leans back in his chair. He mindlessly scrolls up the chat, full of texts and images back and forth. He smiles, going to the top.

2. INT. AUBREY'S APARTMENT - DAY

Suddenly the room is bright, airy and colourful, we're back in time. Arron is excited, bubbling with a now awake and vibrant Aubrey.

AUBREY
OH. MY. GOD. Who is he?!

Arron hides his phone from Aubrey- face flushing red with embarrassment.

ARRON
He's NO ONE Aubrey! Nothing's gonna happen.

Aubrey gushes, jumping on Arron - both laughing.

AUBREY
Arron! I have never seen you with a guy - where did you meet him? What's his name?!

Arron grabs Aubrey's arms, jokingly calming her down.

ARRON
He's not interested. He never will be. Okay?

Aubrey groans, stretching her neck and shaking. Arron laughs and moves away, over to the computer. He sits down.

ARRON
He works in the bagel shop.

He logs onto the computer, Aubrey in the background grabbing her bag, phone, charger, lipstick.

ARRON
And his name is Mitch.

Aubrey looks around, she has everything.

ARRON
Mitchell Barkley.

AUBREY
Ugh. You'll find your Prince Charming someday.

ARRON
Does that make you the Ugly Stepsister?

Aubrey faux gasps, before blowing a kiss moving off and away. Arron thinks, slumbering in the glow of his computer. He leans in and types. We see the computer, he searches the name - and the familiar profile pops up.

A hard cut and it's night, the screen still the same; no messages sent. Arron stares at the screen, considering. He types in 'Hey', and then deletes it. 'Hi'. Deletes. 'Hello!'. Deletes. He leans back, thinking. A door opens behind him and he turns, Aubrey - dressed up -

AUBREY
Don't work too hard. If you finish early text me and I'll let you know where we are. I think Joe's coming!

Arron smiles.

ARRON
Okay. See ya!

Aubrey leaves, shutting the door behind her. Arron pauses, and then, leans back in and types.

ARRON (V.O.)
I'm sure you're more popular than me but in case you're not out tonight, fancy talking?

He hits enter. And waits. He watches the name, 'Mitch: OFFLINE' change to a green dot. Arron sits up, the message changes to 'seen'.

ARRON
Shit.

Then the bubbles.

ARRON
Holy fucking shit.

Ping-

MITCH (V.O.)
Hey anonymous profile. I might fancy talking. But first, A/S/L?

Arron's brows furrow. He pulls up another window and searches A/S/L - the result: Age, Sex, Location.

He smirks, then back to the other page.

ARRON (V.O.)
19. M. UK

His finger hovers over the enter button, before thinking. He deletes.

ARRON (V.O.)
21.

AUBREY (V.O.)
F. UK.

Arron hits enter. It's sent.

3. INT. AUBREY'S APARTMENT - PRESENT DAY
Hard-cut back to the cold, dark room. Arron, illuminated by the computer screen - echoes of the 'OFFLINE' button still aching through him.

ARRON
For fuck's sake.

He stretches his arms up to his head - trying to hide his devastation. When - the green dot returns - ONLINE. Arron sits up, breathing out a shakey breath. Then, a bubbling ringtone as he receives a call. *"Live Videolink with Mitch"*. Arron's face fills with concern, he checks the webcam on his computer - blue tack safely secured.

Arron hovers the cursor over 'accept' before clicking. The video stutters before we see, Mitch, in front of his computer on his phone. He looks up at the webcam.

MITCH
Hey-

He sits forward, looking up at the computer.

MITCH
Hey you. I can't see you.

He waits, Arron filled with dread. He looks over tentatively at Aubrey, still asleep.

MITCH
Hello?

Arron starts typing. "Hey".

MITCH
You don't wanna live chat?

Arron pauses, waiting for Mitch to say something else.

MITCH
Yo I thought you'd wanna see this in real life.

His hands track his torso and over his boxers. Arron gulps in - he does want to. He types: "I'm just nervous x". Mitch's eyes read the message, he smiles wide bright teeth.

MITCH
Oh you're nervous, huh? Do I scare you?

Arron unbuttons the top of his jeans again, hand slowly sinking in.

MITCH
Come on. Put your cam on. I can't just wank over photos of you.

Mitch's hand lazily scrolls around his crotch. Arron watches.

MITCH
God, Aubrey. You're such a fucking slut.

Mitch's neck cranes back - Arron winces - his own hand still in his boxers.

MITCH
But don't worry. I don't count this as cheating.

Arron's brow furrows. He types "Huh?". Mitch smirks-

MITCH
Oh, you're playing dumb! What would your boyfriend think of all we're doing?

Mitch continues a faster pace on camera, Arron's face turns to horror - suddenly realising. He looks over at Aubrey.

MITCH
It's okay. This can be our little secret. What was his name? Jack? Joe? He doesn't have to know. I'm friends with Cassie, think she lives in the same dorm as you, well she was saying you guys had your month anniversary-

In a burst of panic, Arron jumps up and snatches the plug out of the computer - the room descending into darkness. He breathes out -

ARRON
Fuck. No. No.

Arron spins around, hands flying up to his head and clutching his hair. He catches Aubrey, stirring. He buttons up his jeans hurriedly and turns away from her. He breathes sharp, heavy breaths. His hands shake - he clutches the back of the chair, steadying himself as he sobs in the moonlit darkness.

AUBREY
What's going on?

ARRON
I'm fine.

Aubrey stutters up, propping herself against the cushions of the sofa, slurring.

AUBREY
Aw. Why are you crying?

ARRON
I said I'm fucking fine!

He spits, pushing out the chair which crashes into the desk. He grabs his keys and storms out the door.

4. INT. HALLS CORRIDOR - CONTINUOUS
Arron steps into the corridor, door slamming behind him. And then, he collapses back onto the door - tears streaming down his face as he cries, a desperate, silent sob. He slides down the wall until he reaches the floor. He lays his head in his hands and we sharp cut to:

5. INT. HALLS CORRIDOR - CONTINUOUS
The same shot - now brighter - Arron fast asleep against the wall. The door beside him opens and we see someone step out.

CASSIE
Arron. Arron.

Arron jumps awake, looking up.

ARRON
Oh. Hey. What time is it.

CASSIE
It's 7am. Are you locked out?

ARRON
No. No, it's fine. Thanks.

Arron stands up, keys in the door. He escapes her quickly, not giving any eye contact.

6. INT. AUBREY'S APARTMENT - CONTINUOUS

Arron steps into the apartment, on tiptoes. Trying not to wake Aubrey who lays with her back to Arron on the sofa. He steps further in, and we hear a creak of the floorboards.

AUBREY
It's okay Arron, I'm awake.

Aubrey's voice is shakey, almost warbling. Arron stops, as Aubrey turns over - eyes blotchy and red.

AUBREY
Joe broke it off with me.

Arron's stomach drops. What does she know?

ARRON
Joe?

Aubrey sighs, moving her hair from her face.

AUBREY
He said I hooked up with someone last night.

She shakes her head and moves over - signaling for Arron to sit with her.

AUBREY
I just... don't... I don't think I'd do that. Not to him.

Arron sits beside her, but there is a distance.

ARRON
You can't remember?

Aubrey sniffs in, a sigh.

AUBREY
I've fucked it up.

She leans on Arron's shoulder, who reciprocates with a tentative arm around her. He looks at the computer by the wall - can he keep this secret?
We track deep in on him, sharp features cast in shadow - a longing darkness in his eyes.

CREDITS ROLL
END FILM

ARRON

└─→ unexpected predator
└─→ manipulator
└─→ obsessive
└─→ identity crisis.

"I'M SURE YOU'RE MORE POPULAR THAN ME, BUT... FANCY TALKING?"

STARLIGHT

Written: 28 November 2019, Produced: 14 - 15 December 2019

Written by Gage Oxley
Story by Luke Hudson and Gage Oxley

Nathaniel Farah as KANE
James Coutsavlis as JACOB
Callum Hart as MICHAEL

1. INT. KANE'S DORMROOOM - NIGHT

INSERT: Titlecard - "MARCH"

A smokey moonlight filters through in striking sheets as we fade in slowly on an aerial shot of KANE, a 20-year-old man, who lays at a soft angle draped in sheets as crisp white as his boxers.

Slowly, his neck cranes and tilts to the side. He places a bud in his ear. Then, twisting his neck the other way, another bud in another ear.

He breathes out, a dull, heavy breath. We hear every element of the exhale. He stretches out his back, a soft click - the ruffle of the sheets. With eyes shut, Kane's fingers trail across his torso, gliding across his iliac furrow, and over, wrapping his arm around himself in embrace. Then, the camera slowly falls toward him - his inherent beauty filling the frame. Stars begin to trail across the room, first the walls, then the crisp bed-sheets and finally lingering across his body.

His second hand trails up between his chest - up to his neck. His forefinger circles his Adam's apple, then up to his chin - his neck twists again, allowing his finger to trail his jawline. Then, back down as his hand caresses his features. A heavy exhale as we hear skin on skin, feather-filled pillows expressing, a hum at the back of the throat.

As we are excruciatingly close to Kane, his neck stretches and twists. Eyes locking with the camera. Then, the camera rises again, as Kane's hands continue trailing his abdomen. Again, the hair-raising sensations of skin on skin and aching breaths. We are on the high aerial we once started with - Kane's arm that arcs across himself in affection slowly grazes below, digits manipulating the hem of his briefs as they slink beneath, enfolding themselves around a bulge in the material. Kane's open-mouthed expression of pleasure now arcs his gaze to the camera, he watches us.

His second hand cups his chest and advances down his torso and presses down on the hem of the boxers, releasing them around his thighs. Kane's breathing becomes thick and heavy. A spark and the stars glitch, Kane contorts his neck - a sharp projection of a man flexing his biceps. Then, off again, the stars reappear, fainter. He continues sliding his hand up and down, a slightly quicker pace, when - flash - Kane's neck twists again, and another image replaces the sparkling stars - two men in intercourse.

Kane's abdomen dips, an aching breath - a moan - the stars strike back across him - fainter still. His speed increases, a softer moan - a flash of a man performing oral, when bang-
- Kane jumps, scratching and pulling the waistband of his briefs to hike them up - protecting his privacy. He twists and throws himself into the bed, sheets drenching him. We hear keys in the door as it swings open. A young man - JACOB - 21 years old - crashes in, two similar-aged girls, JENNIFER and STEPH following.

We stick on the side profile of Kane as he turns over - eyes open as he holds his shallow breaths. In the out of focus background, Jacob and the girls fumbling onto the bed as we hear muffled kisses and moans. Kane shuts his eyes, trying to shut it out.

INSERT: Titlecard - "STARLIGHT"

2. INT. KANE'S DORMROOM - EARLY EVENING

A quiet, glum and moody setting as a table lit with a harsh high light reflects an interrogation. On the left of the table, Jacob - attractive in the sobering light; in the middle, MICHAEL - 21-years-old, smoking; and on the right Kane. The three play cards, occasionally slapping down a new suit or number mindlessly.

MICHAEL
You want a ciggy?

Michael directs his question to Jacob, who looks up and pulls one out of the packet. Michael turns to Kane-

MICHAEL
Bet you'd love a fag, though, ey?

Kane looks up, hesitating before laughing it off.

KANE
Fuck off.

Michael extends the packet to Kane, who tentatively takes one out.

MICHAEL
You got your dick wet yet, mate?

Kane watches Jacob whose cigarette is already lit and smoking. Kane puts it in his mouth and takes the lighter.

JACOB
Yeah, man. Steph and Jen. Left walkin' funny didn't they Kane?

Kane sucks in on the cigarette, handling awkwardly. He looks up, blowing out. Kane smiles and nods.

KANE
You'd've thought they was getting killed the way they screamed.

Michael laughs, another card down.

MICHAEL
Shit. You get any of Jakey-boy's sloppy seconds?

Kane puts down a card.

KANE
Nah. I can catch my own-

Jacob puts down a card.

JACOB
- and out.

Michael looks up in shock, Kane relieved to have the attention removed.

MICHAEL
How in the fuck? You lucky prick.

3. INT. KANE'S DORMROOM - EVENING
Land on a 1995 episode of Noel's House Party, playing on a small boxed TV stacked
precariously on a handful of boxes that appear as if it wouldn't be able to take the weight.

INSERT: Titlecard - "APRIL"

Kane stretched on his bed, sat upright, writing on paper that has seen better days. Jacob, on
his bed, lent against a stack of pillows - a joint dropping from his mouth, from the glazed look
on his face, we assume it isn't his first.

JACOB
What the fuck even is he?

Kane looks up at Jacob, and follows his gaze to the television. On the screen: Mr Blobby.

JACOB
He looks like a right nonce.

Jacob jumps up and switches the channel. Kane pays no attention, focused on the papers in
front of him. Until, he's disturbed by the sounds of the adult television channel: The Spice
Network.

Jacob stands, walking backwards - not losing gaze of the TV. He drops his tracksuit bottoms,
jumping onto the bed. His hands immediately travel below the hem of his briefs.

Kane continues scribbling, eyes creeping to the side, watching Jacob in his peripherals. Then, his eyes dart back to his work - he cannot be caught. Until, Jacob emits a soft moan, which Kane clocks. He looks over at Jacob, fully now.

KANE
I've got... um... porn?

Jacob looks up, hand slowly shifting out the inside of his boxers, but massaging above the material.

JACOB
Yeah, sure.

Jacob sits back up from his slouched position - he's relaxed compared to Kane's nervous buzz. Kane quickly jumps up and moves over to the TV. He slots in a VHS, as Jacob moves onto the floor beside Kane. The tone of the room changes - a hazier, darker colour. Kane sits back beside Jacob as we hear the soft moans of the video.

Jacob takes another drag of the joint and drops his hand back into his boxers and continues stroking. Jacob offers the joint to Kane, who takes it and hastily inhales, then passes it back to Jacob. Kane stares fixed at the television, then, his own hand stretches into his boxers as he masturbates.

Jacob exhales, a deep groan. Kane looks over, an eye wanders and falls to his crotch before snapping back up. A few beats later, Jacob's hand loses its grip of his own, and without losing gaze on the video reaches over to Kane's lower abdomen, slinking beneath his hem. Kane breathes heavy as Jacob touches him, almost a flinch. Jacob proceeds to stroke Kane, who, hesitantly, reciprocates. His hand longing on his abdomen before gripping his friends' penis. Jacob 'mm's' - as Kane picks up his pace so does his friend. Kane watches his hand move in Jacob's boxers, Jacob stares ahead at the screen, neck craning.

Kane slowly creeps closer to Jacob - and, as the pace escalates Kane looks up at Jacob's face and moves in. Jacob turns, and their lips hit. Jacob immediately retreats, hand whipping out of Kane's briefs. He stands up, hurriedly adjusting himself.

JACOB
What the fuck?!

He grabs his tracksuit bottoms from the floor and quickly pulls them up - then a shirt round himself.

Kane sits, staring ahead - he doesn't say anything. The subtle moans and slapping of the video continues through the quiet scene. Jacob rushes off, over Kane's legs and out through the door, which shuts a little harder than normal behind him.

A moment goes by, Kane's eyes are dead - jawline tight as he tries to hold in his tears.

4. EXT. COUNCIL ESTATE STREET - DAY

Kane walks down the dirty street, flanked by terraced houses. Jacob, a step behind him. The boys walk, no words shared between the pair. Suddenly, a ball rolls into frame. Kane looks up. Three younger boys, around 12, stand. Jumpers on the pathway marking goalposts. Jacob carries on walking, but slows. The ball lands at Kane's feet. He holds it beneath his feet, a moment too long.

BOY 1
Kick it back then, you poof.

Kane looks at him. The boy is cocky, he spits on the floor. Kane passes his gaze to Jacob - who stops and has turned around. Then, Kane turns and blasts the ball down the street, away from the boys.

BOY 2
Eh, what you done that for?

Kane keeps on walking as the boys chase after the ball. He reaches Jacob who carries on walking with him. Jacob looks over his shoulder, watching the kids. He smirks.

JACOB
You feel better now?

They walk, letting the wind pick up missing conversation.

KANE
They fucking deserved it.

Jacob laughs, bright and infectious features.

5. INT. KANE'S DORMROOM - NIGHT

Kane sits on his bed, finger outstretched. The bed opposite him is empty. On the tip of his finger, a tab of blotting paper - an LSD trip. Kane breathes out, exhaling - nervous? Then, quickly he places it on the tip of his tongue and shuts his mouth.

INSERT: Titlecard - "MAY"

|SOUNDTRACK: DAN BLACK feat. KID CUDI - SYMPHONIES (DADA LIFE REMIX) - 01:27 - 2:44|

Now, Kane sat on the floor, back leaning against the bed. He looks up, moonlight washing into his features.

Kane's POV - the oranges and yellows of the room cast by the sodium streetlamps beside their house twinkle and sparkle.

Kane's eyes track them, glossy, wide, taking everything in. He feels it all.

6. EXT. COUNCIL ESTATE STREET - CONTINUOUS
Kane wanders in the street, the crisp May air biting at his skin. He smiles, wide, like the Cheshire cat. Then laughs, properly, with joy and euphoria plastered across his face.

7. EXT. LARGE FIELD - CONTINUOUS
Fireworks blast in the dark draping sky, vibrant colours - pinks, purples and shimmering glitters falling.

Kane watches, the coloured light bouncing across him. When, a hand takes his. He looks down, and then follows the arm up. Jacob, who carries on looking forward, Kane smiles - tearing up.

Behind them, silhouetted against the smoky haze of the firework blast, holding hands while Kane ignores the display to gaze at Jacob.

8. EXT. COUNCIL ESTATE STREET - CONTINUOUS
Kane looks up at the clear stars, mapped in astral light, flinging themselves upon him as he cranes his neck, desperate to be among the divinity. On his feet, as they traverse the bulging cobbles, drenched in pools of May rainwater. Back to his outstretched face, now with starlight tearing below his eyes in Elysian beauty. He comes down, feet back firmly on the ground, as he looks around. He walks - no - glides through the street, stacked terraces either side as he pushes us backwards.

SLAM - a projection hits him, starlight.
He carries on walking.

SLAM - another projection: him, 5-years-old, with his mother.
He carries on walking, but a pained gaze slashes his face.

SLAM - another projection: starlight.
His pace quickens as we move backwards with him.

SLAM - another projection: gay pornography.
He winces, pushing it out of his head, he carries on walking.

SLAM - another projection: him at school, dressed in uniform.
He runs now, the loose cloth of his sleeves wipe his face, yet the starlight remains.

SLAM - another projection: Jacob, shirtless, grinding.
He is disgusted, physically affected.

SLAM - another projection: His father, shouting - echoes of him aching through Kane.
He cries, drained - emotionally and physically.

SLAM - our final projection: Jacob - looking up, fingers hooked on the hem of his briefs as he pulls them low, before- BLACK.

9. INT. KANE'S DORMROOM - DAY

A fan oscillates, blowing paper streamers on the metal corrugation as we pan around their room - a warm glow among the burnt ambers of the hot sky. A blue glow emits from a small television still propped precariously by books and boxes. Kane and Jacob sit in front of the television, controllers in hand as they hurriedly press buttons.

INSERT: Titlecard - "JUNE"

The two are sat on the floor in only briefs - another fan close in front of them as they lurch their arms and bodies engaged in the videogame.

KANE
What was that spawn?! Yo, this is so rigged.

Jacob laughs, carrying on playing while Kane drops his controller and lies down on the floor.

KANE
One life left, mate.

Kane breathes out, stretching his back as it clicks. He exhales, basking in the warm summer glow which drips across his skin.

JACOB
You need to get on my level.

Kane smiles.

KANE
The only reason you're good is cause you're so high.

JACOB
Exactly. Eat acid, beat Super Mario.

Kane groans.

KANE
It's so fucking hot.

There's a silence as Jacob continues clicking ferociously.

JACOB
Have you ever got off with a lad?

The question shocks Kane, who remains laid down. His features tense.

KANE
No.

1st assistant director, Alex Bamford, helped re-write this scene on-set. An avid gamer, and fan of the 90's era, he supported the terminology change to reflect Mortal Kombat 5.

But he's waited too long to say it, and he's said the wrong thing, hasn't he? Kane's mind races, a celestial explosion behind glazed eyes. When, a flash on the screen disturbs Jacob's stillness.

JACOB
Shit.

He plants the controller down.

JACOB
I'm dead.

Jacob turns around at Kane.

JACOB
Listen -

He sniffs in heavily, rubbing his nose.

JACOB
When we was wanking, why'd you... you know.

Kane remains laying down. Staring at the ceiling. There's a pause, a soft stillness carried by the white noise of the fans.

KANE
I think-

Kane now looks over at Jacob.

KANE
I dunno. I guess I wanted to. To know what it felt like.

Jacob turns away now, picking his fingernails.

JACOB
Are you a homo?

There's a pause, no answer. Jacob turns around, as soon as he catches Kane's gaze, Kane answers.

KANE
No. Well, I don't think so.

Jacob turns back. Kane sighs, sitting up now.

KANE
I've never kissed a lad before. That's why. And... we was messing around... I just thought-

Jacob turns round, interrupting Kane and pushing into him, kissing him tentatively. Jacob pushes Kane down, arms either side of him as he leans above him, becoming an intimidating force.

Jacob picks up a joint from the side of the cabinet beside him and lights it, toking on it before placing it back down. He exhales a cloud of deep smoke, and then, slithers down Kane's body. An over the shoulder of Jacob as we see his head slowly bob below camera. Kane breathes heavy, head falling back.

10. INT. KANE'S DORMROOM - EARLY EVENING
A hard cut into the early evening as the two lads lay entangled in each other. Kane is out of it, breathing heavy - eyes closed. Jacob looks around, and we pull focus on a bud on the bedside counter. Jacob sits up, softly pushing his friend off of him as he quietly moves over. He trivially grinds it into a roll-up as he sprinkles some tobacco over it.

He breathes out, as he crafts it, he looks over at Kane sleeping on the floor. He stops, a momentary pause, drenched with guilt, shame, embarrassment. He rolls it round, licking the paper, then placing it in his mouth.

11. INT. KANE'S DORMROOM - DAY
The room, now scarcer than it was before, is piled with boxes - marked 'Kane'. Kane looks around the room, last checks.

INSERT: Titlecard - "JULY"

The door opens, Jacob enters. He stands in the doorway, looking around.

JACOB
Shit. You leaving now?

Kane places his final box on the floor, looking up at Jacob.

KANE
Back to me da's. Then...

He trails off, not knowing where his life is taking him.

JACOB
Yer could always stick around. I mean. It's been good, mate. You're a sound lad an'... I dunno.

Kane looks at Jacob.

KANE
It's been good? It's been good? That's it is it? Fuck me.

Kane retreats to his boxes. Jacob's face falls, hard features -

JACOB
What the fuck else am I meant to say, eh?

Jacob moves away from the door now, close to Kane.

JACOB
You want me to say how much I liked seein' you spaff over me?

KANE
Fuck off, Jacob.

Kane turns away, focused on the boxes.

JACOB
Or ... the kick I got fuckin' you like a fag?

Kane stands now,

KANE
I said fuck off!

Kane quickly slams his fist into Jacob whose head cracks backwards. There's a silence between the pair until Jacob closes the gap. Kane, quiet bar his breathing, not intimidated until Jacob moves closer in and kisses him. Kane struggles to wriggle free.

KANE
You're mental, mate. You fuckin' high now, yeah?

Jacob looks at Kane, face cold, void of emotion.

KANE
'cos that's the only time you ever do owt.

Kane sighs, hands flying up to his hair.

KANE
Fuck sake. You wreck my head, like.

He picks up another box, moving it, before collapsing on the bed.

KANE
I feel fuckin' sick. An' I get it. I get why you have to have a spliff or... whatever. 'Cos if you feel anythin' like I do, I'd want to be fuckin' numb. So. I do get it, like. But I can't keep doin' this. I'm not that lad.

Kane hurriedly wipes the tears from his eyes, determined not to show weakness. Jacob exhales, looks around the room.

JACOB
I'm not that lad either. Maybe that's the problem.

There's two muffled beeps from a car outside the house, the two look up at the window. Kane stands, feverishly drying his eyes.

KANE
Tha's me da.

Kane sighs. He didn't want it to end like this. There's a beat.

KANE
If... if you ever become that lad. Find me, won't you.

Jacob runs his hands through his hair and turns around, opening the door for Kane.

JACOB
Yer da's waiting.

Kane nods, breathing out through his nose, holding it together. He grabs a box and moves out of the door. Jacob, a step behind him - grabs another box as he walks through the door.

CREDITS ROLL
END FILM

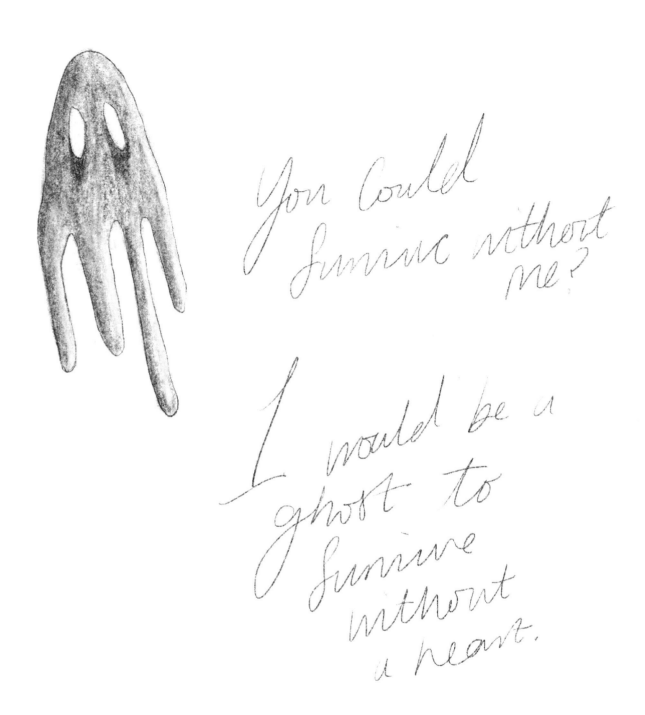

You Could Survive without me?

I would be a ghost to survive without a heart.

"YOU COULD SURVIVE WITHOUT ME?" - I WOULD BE A GHOST WITHOUT A HEART

While in the process of writing the screenplay, I would often have these little sketches and bursts of ideas that sometimes made it to the final version. Perhaps the above was just outside the scouse lads' vernacular.

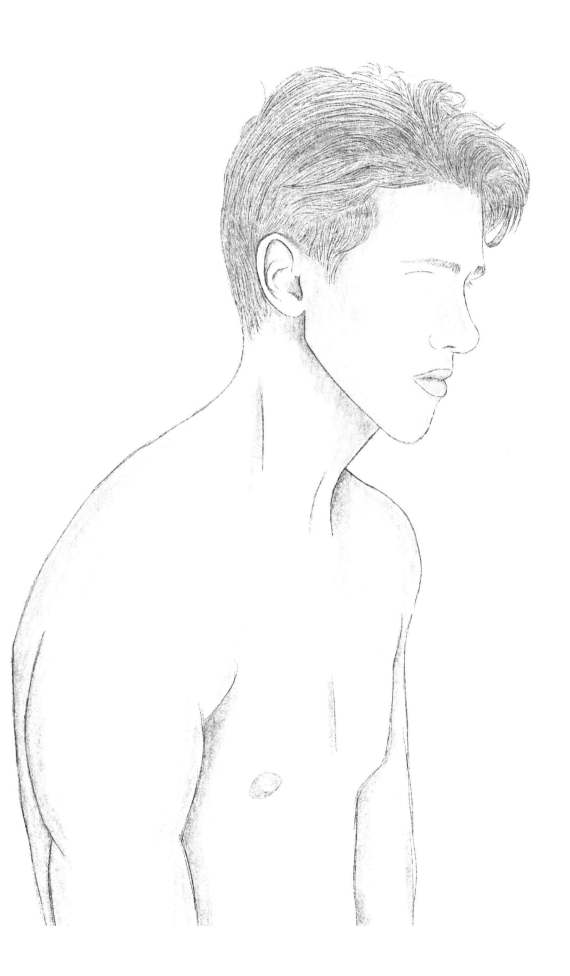

BLACKLIGHT

Written: 30 December 2019, Produced: 11 - 13 January 2020

Written by Gage Oxley
Story by Charlie Harris and Gage Oxley

Charlie Harris as ADAM
Nadhía Porcelli as ALEXIA
Julia Goodinson as DAPHNE

1. INT. ADAM'S BEDROOM - NIGHT
A young man, ADAM is laid on his bed, moonlight spilling across the draping white bed-sheets. His face is illuminated by a cold glow from the screen of his phone. He wears a white t-shirt close to his skin and a pair of boxers.

His thumb flies across the screen as he scrolls down a photo-sharing social media platform. Then, he stops, scrolls back, to a girl. Adam swallows, a subconscious tick. He presses on the girls page and suddenly his phone is swarmed with images of her in various forms of undress - holiday photos, nights out. He presses on one particular image - teasing. Then, his other hand trails down and above his boxers. Slow at first as we see his eyes glued to the picture. He zooms with one hand, and grips with his other.

To the phone, he scrolls through various photos, quick, zooming in and out. He cranes his neck up, spluttering breaths, and back to the pictures - mouth open and breathing heavy. Then, semen seeps through the front of his boxers as his stroking slows. His breath still heavy. His hand slinks away from the wet boxers, movement tentative as not to spoil his shirt or sheets. His phone still blaring images of the girl, Adam scrolls back to the top and we see her name: ALEXIA FORD, a blue tick beside it. Then: Influencer. Followers: 49k

He pauses a moment longer, space quiet bar his subtle breaths. A tattered teddy bear wearing a red varsity jacket lays beside the bed - Adam looks at it, before scratching its head.
He presses the 'Message' button and types quickly. "Hey. I would love to meet you, I think we'd get on well. Can I treat you to a coffee?" Send.

Then, he stretches upwards, back cracking - he stands up and as he hits the door of his room, he pulls his boxers down and drops them in the bin beside the dresser.

TITLE CARD: BLACKLIGHT

2. INT. ADAM'S BEDROOM - DAY
The room is a hazy quiet, a sense of security wraps around the scene in its warm lighting. We hit on a handful of objects: a belt strewn over the bedhead, a tape dispenser mixed with other stationary, a DSLR camera - a good one - with a telephoto lens. Then, a hand on a glossy white computer mouse, fingers clicking mindlessly. Onto Adam's eyes - focused, two white screens reflecting back in his eyes. In front of him, his desktop spaced between two screens - on one: a promotional poster photo of "CALI X", seemingly a pop star, modeling provocatively, protecting her modesty with a large teddy bear.

On the other screen, a close up of her face. Her neck being recoloured expertly by Adam. He sits up, clicks his fingers methodically - one, two, three, four. Then, he zooms out of the screen as we see the celebrity's face has been edited onto a pornographic image. Adam leans forward, scanning each and every detail.

The screen is replaced by a website: "UNDERCOVERS": Male Forum. Adam drags his creation over onto the page, and, once its uploaded - we see a preview of the final render: a fully moving, artificial intelligence-created deepfake. Adam watches it, rubbing the sleep from his eyes. Then, a ping, as a notification comes in. Adam smirks, leaning forward - a message from "MASTERFAKE" reads 'your the pro blacklight.' and another 'fuckkk she needs to get on her knees and worship me'.

Adam smiles, laughs - his face filled with actual glee. He leans forward and closes the windows, as soon as his face reflects the dark light from the monitor his features fall. No more smile.

3. INT. ADAM'S KITCHEN - EVENING
Adam walks from the kitchen with two plates - brimming with food. He plants it in front of his grandmother, DAPHNE.

ADAM
For the madame.

Daphne looks up and chuckles,

DAPHNE
You're too good.

Adam sits down at the table, his own plate in front of him.

ADAM
Well, you raised me right.

Daphne's smile falters slightly, she inhales - something not been spoken.

DAPHNE
One day you'll make a girl very happy.

ADAM
One day? More like one year. One decade.

Daphne tuts,

DAPHNE
You keep telling yourself that, you never will! What about the lassies at your work?

Adam looks up, clocking his grandmother -

51

ADAM
It's .. um .. mostly guys who work there. And we don't really get to engage with the celebs.

DAPHNE
Oh! Yes. My Adam with a celebrity. That's what you deserve, love.

Adam smiles,

ADAM
Yeah. Yeah, that'd be nice.

There's a beat as Adam spools his food.

ADAM
There is this girl. I'm thinking of working with. She's ... semi-famous. Alexia.

DAPHNE
Oh? Are you thinking of courting?

ADAM
Courting?! No. No. Maybe an article on her.

DAPHNE
You should! Give her a platform. If you promoted her, think of how much that'd help her out. Girls love a man who can help them.

Adam nods, mulling it over. He resumes his eating.

DAPHNE
Speaking of, Lisa next door asked if we can look after their dog while she's out Saturday next week. You'll be around to take him for a walk, won't you?

Adam nods, chewing his food.

ADAM
Yeah. Sure.

4. INT. ADAM'S BEDROOM - NIGHT

Adam's computer screens are dominated by "UNDERCOVERS". Various tabs show a variety of threads: 'Quality Content', 'Inceldom in the News and Media', 'Celebrities', 'Blackpill', 'Natural Foids' and 'Memes'

Adam clicks on 'Celebrities', and then quickly on 'New Post'. He pauses on the subject line before typing 'ALEXIA FORD'.

He cranes his head back, leaning against his desk chair. He exhales, slow, contained before sitting back up and pressing 'Submit'. Seconds later, the thread has started. He smiles, shutting his eyes, imagining the result. He opens a drawer beside his bed and pulls out a pre-rolled joint. A flick of the lighter as sparks drench the twisted end in flame as it burns. As he smokes, he stands up from the desk and stands in front of a long mirror. He stares deep at himself in the reflection, before shifting - posing - he watches himself blow a cloud of smoke and then, his hand rubbing against his jawline and down his neck, circling his Adam's Apple, down his chest and torso and to the front of his jeans. He holds himself while watching - eyes deep, watery, pained. His hand trails back up over his chest and towards his arms. He caresses his shoulder and down to his bicep. He holds his arm out, flexing - he strains his face, breathing heavy. He releases his muscles while toking on the joint.

He tries again, flexing - disappointed in the result - veins protruding in his forehead, neck stretching, his face becoming flushed. Still, no good. He exhales quickly and heavily, face torn with anger. He pulls his t-shirt off, mercilessly stretching and clawing at the material. He throws the joint on the floor before flexing again, both arms this time.

ADAM
Fuck you.

He spits, odious, ashamed.

ADAM (screaming)
FUCK YOU. FUCK YOU.

5. INT. ADAM'S LIVING ROOM - CONTINUOUS
The muffled shouts of Adam are heard above the roof as Daphne sits in her armchair, blanket draped over her.

6. INT. ADAM'S BEDROOM - CONTINUOUS
Adam calms himself down. Staring with dull eyes at his reflection. As his breathing slows, we hear a plink of a notification. He turns, like a moth drawn to flame, Adam moves towards the computer. He sits down and on the screen: a reply from a user. *"She's such a slut, man. I've seen what she does off camera. Here bro."*

Beside the message is a link - Adam hesitantly drags the arrow over it. His eyes roam the wall, searching for a distraction? A way out? Click. His monitor is filled with personal and private thumbnails, photos and videos. Adam leans forward, the array of flesh reflected in his eyes. He smiles, an unsettling slither akin to the Cheshire cat.

7. INT. ADAM'S HALLWAY - DAY
Another knock on the door, hurried, loud. A dog barks. Adam races down the staircase as Daphne opens the door.

ADAM
It's mine. I'll get it.

Daphne is pushed aside, in front of a flustered delivery driver.

DAPHNE
Don't let the bloody dog out.

DELIVERY DRIVER
Adam Mason?

ADAM
Yep.

He grabs the package hurriedly, about to close the door.

DELIVERY DRIVER
I need it signed for.

Adam sighs, grabbing the device and scribbling on it. He passes it back to the driver and shuts the door.

8. INT. ADAM'S BEDROOM - MOMENTS LATER

Adam kneels up on his bed, the box in front of him. He breathes out, exhaling a shaky breath. In his hand, a Stanley knife. He gently presses the blade into the tape at the sides, creeping it down with immaculate precision. At last, the roof's pressure expires and Adam carefully unfurls the tab. He raises it up - and reveals inside - a black hardback photobook. He caresses the cover, lifting it up from the blood red tissue below it. He opens the cover and in the middle, a clear photo: Alexia Ford.

He places the book down on the bed, now tossing the box aside carelessly. He stands up on the bed. Looking down at the portrait within the book. He looks around the room, spots what he's after, and jumps down onto the floor. He grabs a roll of cling film and returns to the bed, he pulls sheets of the plastic wrap from its container and layers it over the mattress of the bed. He obsessively layers, ripping and tearing sheets spitting through gritted teeth. He throws the box of plastic wrap which skids across the floor and lands beside a cabinet, stacked with identical black photobooks.

Adam surveys the book like prey, now atop a fully cling-filmed mattress. He clicks his belt off, threading it through the hooks on his trousers, once loose he drops them to the floor, stepping out of the legs. He moves over to the bed, again kneeling up above the book. He wraps the belt over his neck, hooking the latch through as he clears his throat, stretched by the leather.

With one hand he lifts the cover revealing more images of Alexia. He breathes heavy. The other hand tightening the free strand of the belt. His face already tinting with redness. Now, his other hand lifts from the book and slips into his boxers. He gasps, from the touch or from the loss of air. He slides his hand back and forth within his underwear, a painfully slow, aching pull. He views every photo with intensity. Placing himself among them.

Then, turns the page with the hand in his boxers, then as it returns he pushes them down and off. He never loses grip of the belt tight around his neck.

Then, a bark and a scratch at the door - Adam's concentration falters as he slips slightly, looking toward the door. But, he regains his pace and stares at the set of new photos. His hand moving slightly quicker in his trousers which have gently fallen from his erratic movement.

Another bark, more eager, desperate. Adam stares forward at the book but we can tell he's angry. His fury building inside him. He quickens his pace, turning another page, he moans but it's choked by the belt. His face dripping with beads of sweat as his hand shakes below camera. He is getting close. Another bark, scratching becoming frantic. He moans again, arcing his back but never losing focus of the photos as he cums, his face red and sweaty with lust and disgust. He breathes out thick heavy breaths - at the peak. Another bark, louder and harsher. He snaps, the belt releasing - standing up from the bed and dashing off camera, more barking as he leaves frame and we stick on the bed. We hear the door open, the muffled barks turning clear as the barrier between the dog and us opens. But, the barking quickly turns, a dull hit and the dog whines, another hit and another whine. Then, the door slams.

[MUSIC: SMELLS LIKE TEEN SPIRIT - PATTI SMITH]

A pause, long and aching. What the fuck happened?

Adam enters back into frame, slowly. He stands beside the bed, loose shirt, damp boxers and the belt now slack around his neck which has an impression of the leather strap.

He moves over to the desk, picking up the DSLR. He plays with the buttons, tapping the side, thinking. He turns - towards the bed. He looks at mattress, the photobook above the drenched cling film. He flicks the lamp beside his bed off, washing the room in the warm sodium streetlamps from his window. He stands on the bed, the plastic wrap cracking beneath his feet. He leans up, and clicks a button beside a box above his bed. Then, the room erupts in a blue wash - as he turns the blacklight on. At first we see the glow on Adam's hands which grip the camera - he examines the first, stringing between fingers. Then, the second, marred across his knuckles. He realises what it is. He smiles. Then he drops his hand and looks down, his wry smile turning into a full on laugh. Maniacal and genuinely gleeful as we see what he sees: the bed, with glowing sprays, across the photobook containing images of Alexia.

He readies his camera, and snaps a photo. He examines his artwork, lips furl as he smiles, eyes glowing with a pure high.

He breathes out, stretching, craning his neck - as he moves his head down we spot something else, glowing with muffled matter. His brows furrow in confusion. He switches the blacklight off, returning the darkened state to its normal warm daylight. Where his gaze upon the once glowing item reveals the tattered, old, innocent teddy bear. He exhales, jumping off the bed and towards the bear. He picks it up, thinking.

9. INT. ADAM'S KITCHEN - DAY

Adam sits at the counter, earphones in - watching a new video featuring Alexia and another girl. He looks up, seeing Daphne with a murky red cloth, being cleaned at the sink. His face void of emotion as his attention returns to the video.

DAPHNE
Honestly. Some people. I despair.

Daphne shakes her head.

DAPHNE
This world. I don't recognise half of it any more.

Adam focuses intently on the video, wide eyes eating every detail. We hear the video through his earphones:

ALEXIA
- it really would mean the world to me and Carrie, and we really hope to meet you there! So. Carrie. We're going to do something I've wanted to do for a long time.

Adam sits forward, inhaling through his nose - controlled but heavy.

CARRIE
That's right! We're going to go through your fan messages and respond to them!

ALEXIA
Now, I haven't seen any of these before - so I'm seeing them for the first time just like you guys!

The video cuts, and the pair are now on a split screen, the right hand side taken up with a screen record of her phone. The first message, from a fan, is read by Alexia.

ALEXIA
Aw! Isn't this just the cutest. @AlexiaStan04 says "Hey Lexi, I've watched you for years and what you do for girls like me means everything! I love you!". Well, AlexiaStan, I love you too!

Adam bites his nails, a breathy laugh, he sees the bullshit.

ALEXIA
Ooh! This next one is from a boy - he says "Hey. I would love to meet you, I think we'd get on well. Can I treat you to a coffee?"

Adam's face falters, emotion bleeding through. His heart beats. That's his message.

CARRIE
Oooh! Alexia has a date!

ALEXIA
I wouldn't go that far-

CARRIE
Look at his profile!

Carrie reaches across and presses the icon, the screen is covered by blurred images.

ALEXIA
Oh my God!

Carrie laughs,

CARRIE
He's cute!

ALEXIA
Yeah... he is. Um, but politely - it's a pass.

Carrie tries grabbing Alexia's phone, who slides it back to her messages.

ALEXIA
We'll blur your name for posterity.

CARRIE
Posterity? He doesn't need posterity, he needs a date!

ALEXIA
Well, he isn't going to get one from me-

The video goes black as we cut to the real world, and Adam slams the laptop lid shut. Daphne turns.

DAPHNE
Adam!

Adam stands, picking up the laptop and slamming it on the table - he screams, spitting and shouting as the laptop splinters.

DAPHNE
Adam! Adam! Stop it!

He eventually does, breathing out - he runs fingers through his hair as he sees what he's done. Daphne is against the wall, cowering. He pauses for a moment, shakes his head and leaves.

10. INT. ADAM'S BATHROOM - LATER

Adam stands in front of his mirror, he stares at himself - examining every detail. Then, he lifts a razor up to his head and scrolls it over his hair as it falls away. He stares deep into the mirror, another round of shaving. His eyes deep, glassy.

11. INT. ADAM'S BEDROOM - LATER

Adam packs a carry-all, throwing items in hurriedly. He looks around his room - he spots the belt, swinging on the back of the chair. He picks it up and runs his fingers over it. Then, gently embraces himself as he wraps it around his waist. Circling the metal clutch as he secures it. He leaves, taking the carry-all with him, revealing the childhood teddy bear torn, ripped in shreds across the floor.

12. EXT. ADAM'S HOUSE - EARLY EVENING

Adam's car boot is open, he throws the carry-all in and shuts the boot, heading over to the driver's seat. Daphne, looking helplessly out of the window. Adam shuts the car door as he starts the engine, and drives off.

13. INT. CAFE / MEETING SPACE - MORNING

Adam pushes through a door into a crowded space, mostly filled with teen-age girls. He slinks through them, engaged in busy conversation. An over the shoulder, as the expansive room filled with bustling people is out of focus. He moves through the crowd, until the lights change and the focus pulls - Alexia Ford, standing up onto a makeshift stage. She taps a microphone.

ALEXIA
Oh. My. God. Hello guys!

There's a rambunctious response from the room as Alexia laughs. Adam has stopped, he doesn't react amongst the gaggle of screaming girls.

ALEXIA

I never thought I'd see so many of you here! I cannot wait to meet you all in the signing after I read you an exclusive chapter of my new book!

She sits down on a stool and readies herself. Adam now moves forward, slowly. We track down as we see his fingers brush the clasp of his belt, loosening and then tightening it. He sits at a spare spot at the front, right in front of her. She flicks her hair behind her shoulder. Looking around the settling room. She locks eyes with Adam.

ALEXIA
We all ready?

She chuckles, opening her book. Adam's cold face then turns, twisting, slowly, as if hooking either side of his mouth and pulling upward. A fake, manufactured and hideous smile.

CREDITS ROLL
END FILM

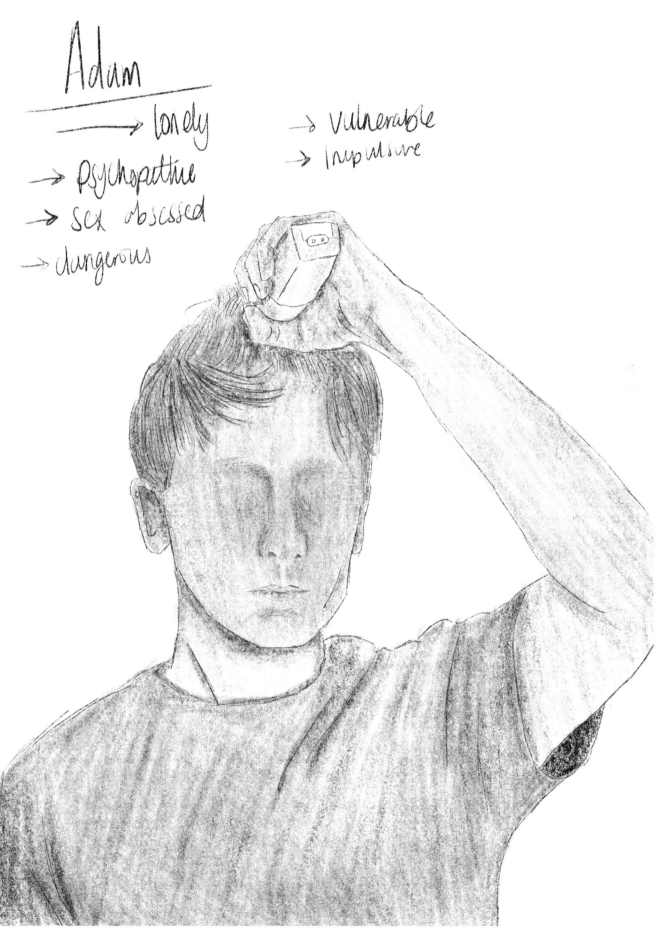

THE DESIGN OF THE FRONT COVER OF INFLUENCER AUTHOR ALEXIA
FORD'S NOVEL "STOP GHOSTING ME". PRODUCERS HAD TO PRINT
SEVERAL PHYSICAL COPIES OF THE BOOK AS A PROP, YOU CAN READ
THE UNSEEN INTERIOR ON PAGE 92.

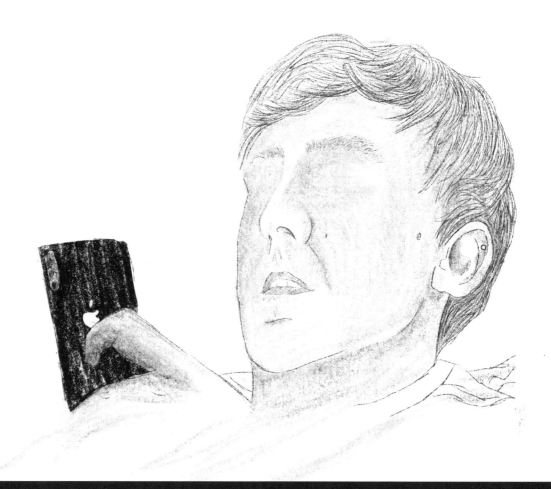

INCELS, AND THE DANGER THEY POSE, ARE VERY MUCH AT THE FOREFRONT OF "BLACKLIGHT". AS A RELATIVELY UNKNOWN SUB-CULTURE, WRITERS CHARLIE HARRIS AND GAGE OXLEY HAD TO VENTURE INTO THESE 'COMMUNITIES', POSING AS INCELS TO GAIN INSIGHT AND NARRATIVE GUIDANCE, UNKNOWN TO OTHER USERS.

LIMELIGHT

Written: 20 January 2020 (Revised 30 May 2020), Produced: 8 - 9 June 2020

Written by Gage Oxley (with additional dialogue from Estelle Herbelin-Earle)
Story by Bruce Herbelin-Earle and Gage Oxley

Bruce Herbelin-Earle as NILS   Charlie Phillips as MATT
Rebecca Whittle as SAIRA   Jacob Holdsworth as MICHAEL(A)
Ash Patel as CRAIG   Estelle Herbelin-Earle as MAMAN

1. INT. AUDITION ROOM - DAY

Start on a man. Hollow cheeks and glassy eyes. He stares at the camera as we pull away.

NILS
- and crashes in blows against the jagged rock. Spikes slam and crack the frothing wash, bent, braking together in harmony.

A pause. Silence. He exhales after a moment, shaky.

The other side of the room now - four people, three of which furiously looking down and scribbling notes. The fourth, a man on the end, stares forward. The woman next to him leans in and whispers in his ear. He remains staring forward.

CRAIG
Ok. Brilliant.

He scans the paper in front of him.

CRAIG
Nils? Ok.

Craig pushes the glasses up his head, resting in his hair.

CRAIG
I think that's everything from us. We'll be in touch.

Nils adopts his perfected poker face. He opens his mouth, but the woman next to Craig, Saira, couldn't cut in quick enough.

SAIRA
Well, thank you very much. Let me show you out.

She stands, Nils watches and follows her out.

INSERT - Titlecard: LIMELIGHT

LIMELIGHT

INT. CITY BUS - DAY
[Scene performed in French dialogue]

Nils watches out of the window, earphones in, the scenery pulling alongside him as the bus flies. He looks down, to the phone in his lap which holds a caller ID: Maman.

Nils holds a moment, biting his lip. His finger toys over the red decline before tapping to accept the call.

NILS
Hi Mum.

MAMAN
What's wrong?

A pause, she hears something in his voice.

NILS
Nothing, I'm fine. Doing great at the moment.

Another pause. Nils knows he's been caught out.

MAMAN
How was the audition?

NILS
I don't know, good I suppose.

MAMAN
Good, like you're going to be chosen for the role?

Nils rolls his eyes, returning his gaze to the passing scene.

NILS
I don't know mum. I did my thing and now I wait for them to call me.

MAMAN
You've been waiting two years for a call. When are you going to start making some money? How long do you think we're going to be paying your rent? That kind of money doesn't grow on trees.

He bites his nails, grimacing

MAMAN
Your father and I have been talking; we want you to come home. Your situation is making us depressed. We have decided not to renew the lease on your apartment this month. When you get here, you'll be working alongside your father at the quarry until you're able to support yourself.

Nils stops a moment, his heart plummets.

NILS
You're joking. Are you serious, mum?

MAMAN
Very serious.

NILS
You think I'm not trying hard enough, is that it?

MAMAN
Maybe you should consider something different, something you're better suited to. Go back to school, maybe? At the moment, you're not proving to us that you are determined, and that you want it enough. You know, this life isn't for everyone.

NILS
What do you want me to do, mum? Waltz back in there and demand the fucking role?

MAMAN
I don't give a shit. I'm putting you on a plane and you're coming home.

NILS (louder)
But... give me... It's my life, you can't do this!

MAMAN
You'll be able to live your proper life once you stop draining ours. It's final. I'll be sending your flight details tomorrow morning.

NILS
Mum? MUM?

As he tries to retort, he is too late - his mother has hung up. His eyes glisten, tears on the verge, longing to fall. He rips his earphones out. He seethes, jaw clenching, teeth biting the inside of his mouth. A moment passes before he jumps up and rings the bell.

3. INT. AUDITION ROOM - LATER
A new man, same hollowed cheeks, eerily similar in looks to Nils, stands in front of the camera now.

MATT
I'm nothing, right. You hear me? You ever stop and think, how fucking... wrong it is... to tell people they're special. My mom told me that every day. But she doesn't know anything. I'm a fucking dime a-

-there's an opening of a door to the side of the frame. Matt is distracted, he looks over. Nils walks into the room.

MATT
- dime a dozen.

Matt stumbles, he's lost. What does he do? The panel look up in bewilderment.

SAIRA
Excuse me, you need to wait outside.

NILS
You need to see me now.

SAIRA
Listen, I know we're running late - but this is not a good first impression.

Saira's unknowing words hit Nils hard. There's a beat.

MATT
Shall I continue?

The man on the end of the casting panel squints, brows furrowing. He recognises Nils.

NILS
- you need to see me. Now. Please.

Saira stands, Craig lightly holds her arm.

CRAIG
One moment.

SAIRA
Can we get someone to escort this man out?

Saira looks to the quiet panel members to her right.

NILS
- you need to see me.

MATT
Come on, dude.

Matt is exasperated. Saira is coming round the side of the table.

CRAIG
Hang on, Saira.

SAIRA
It's time to leave. Come on.

NILS
Please. You need to see me.

CRAIG
I'm really sorry, sir, this doesn't usually happen-

SAIRA
We've seen you, okay. We've seen you now.

MATT
It's okay, it just threw me.

Saira is nearing Nils.

NILS
Don't touch me. Please. Give me a chance. Just see me.

SAIRA
This really isn't okay, now.

Nils backs up, cornered.

NILS
Please.

Craig stands now,

CRAIG
Thanks for your patience.

SAIRA
That's enough.

Saira's hand outstretches to guide Nils away, but he's quicker. His hand delves into his coat pocket and he slowly reveals a single-action revolver.

NILS
Please.

SAIRA
Oh shit.

MATT
What the fuck, man?!

CRAIG
Saira?

Nils holds the gun outward, other hand supporting his shaking arm.

NILS
Sit. Down.

Saira's hands are up, she backs slowly.

SAIRA
Just, let's... calm down.. okay? Everybody. Just breathe.

NILS
I want to fucking audition.

Saira continues walking backwards, she collides with the table. Craig, still standing, pulls her round.

CRAIG
Okay. Okay. Let's do it.

Saira sits down. Breathing sharp and heavy, Craig still stands, but he's low - cowering, he's lost control.

Matt makes a move, shifting towards the door. Nils shifts his arm, pointing it directly at Matt. The other woman on the casting panel, Michaela, gasps.

MICHAELA
Oh my god.

NILS
Don't move.

Matt holds his hands up, moving backwards.

MATT
Okay, alright.

Nils lowers his backpack onto the floor.

NILS
Sit there.

He points his gun to a radiator against the wall. Matt turns, looking, and back to Nils.

MATT
Sure thing.

Matt cautiously retreats, hands still up and sits against the radiator. Nils rummages in his bag, and pulls out a zip tie. He moves over to Matt.

NILS
Hands.

MATT
I'm not gonna go anywhere, mate.

Nils looks up at Matt, his eyes are desperate, full of hunger.

NILS
Hands.

Nils is stern, controlled, careful. But his hands still shake as he zip ties Matt to the radiator. It's awkward and clunky - we know he's not done this before.

MATT (whispering)
Listen man, I get it, right. I've been there. But this isn't the way.

Nils continues zip tying, inhaling sharply through his nose. He hears Matt, but tries to ignore him. Matt looks away, he's done what he can. Nils returns to the center of the room. He exhales. Then, looks up to the panel. The fourth panel member, a young man, face a ghostly white and wide eyes stumbles up, pressing the camcorder beside the panel. He sits back down and nods.

Nils stares ahead,

NILS
Nils Grinstead. 23. London.

It's like a switch, face a subtle luminescence. He turns, one side, turns, second side. Revolver still gripped tightly in his hand. He relaxes his shoulders, stands on the 'X', stares ahead.

NILS
This is the change. Not the loose coins you deny to the half-dead drifters that litter paths and park benches. It's the change that fuels my aching hunger. Look at life. What it teaches us: out with the old, in with the new. Age paralyses dictators and governments that clutch too much power for too long. But look where we are. This constant of hedonism. In with the old. Out with the new. You get so sick that you don't even notice the homeless anymore. They're just filthy spectres. You know who scares the living shit out of you, though? It's the ones who survive, who can still fight, run, hide, think. And, you know they hate you. They're the ones you look out for on the streets. Men like me, who can scratch your ankles. So what do you do? You shoot our fingers. That's why I stay focused. Why I am a fucking psycho. I ravage my sanity before you can. You screw me, because I'm a nobody. I'm nothing, right? You hear me? You ever stop and think, how fucking wrong it is to tell people they're special. My mum told me that every day. But she doesn't know anything. I'm a fucking dime a dozen. That's why I carry a gun: to stand out. Guns mend imbalance quickly. But you know the most refined weapon? Fear. The results are breath-taking. And, you know, it's not bound to bodies. I can take on institutions, organisations, powers and democracies.

68

Fear knows there's no intermission from terror. Of course it gathers quilts and draws society like moths to flame. I know you do, too: dwell on disaster. You crave victims. Voyeur over serial killers, fulfilling your allocation of stimulation. You're sentimental over starving infants, the illiterate little children of the scrapyards. So throw me out. Kick me when I'm down. Leave me to rot. It'll all burn one day. And it's gonna fucking blaze. Torch the system, ignite the poor, burn down this democracy that rapes you over and over. Look at me! Free admission, open daily, everyone's prostitute. The flames of my cunt devour the privileged. The apocalypse is blooming. I collect the skulls lain from bombs, scavenging through the ashes. I fuck their heads like they can fit me, tables overturned. But it's not enough. And so I crash it in blows against the jagged rock. Spikes slam and crack the frothing wash, bent, braking together in harmony.

Throughout his monologue, Nils escalates, spitting with later syllables and a shaking fury in his lungs. The prose shifts mid-way, the panel become discomforted. Is this the script? Is this his aching reality?

When he finishes, he breathes out. Scratches the back of his head with the hand that holds the revolver. Saira leans into Craig, murmuring something in his ear. He nods.

CRAIG
Listen-

NILS
Did you not hear me?

Craig's mouth shuts closed. He swallows.

CRAIG
We did, and... it was impressive.

NILS
I need this.

CRAIG
I know. Just. Drop the gun.

Nils fingers the gun, letting it roam across his palm. He shakes his head.

NILS
Who wrote that monologue?

Craig looks to Saira, do they answer?

SAIRA
Um... it was a lady called-

NILS
Are they here?

Another pause.

SAIRA
No. She's not.

Nils looks up at the panel.

NILS
Then I need you to know, each one of you has done this.

He holds the revolver to his other open palm and fires, a deafening crack of the bullet as blood engulfs in quick flame. Nils' hand is dripping red, sinew and bone. He screams, as do the panel. Michaela stands, instant -

MICHAELA
What the fuck are you doing?!

CRAIG
Don't. Michaela.

Nils, crippled on his knees puts the gun back to his hand and fires again, another scream from the room. Matt, in the corner, shields his face.

MICHAELA
Stop it, please!

Nils' face is creased in pain. He drops the gun, holding his crimson fist.

NILS
Are you going to offer me the role?

His voice aches, warbling. The panel is quiet, cold. Their silence speaks volumes.
Nils nods, exhales. He stands, swaying away from the gun. He moves over to Matt, hands tight in the zip-tie.

MATT
Please, no, please - is it money? I have money. How much do you want?

He stops as soon as Nils' delicately brushes both hands up Matt's cheeks.

NILS
It's not enough.

Then, slam. He cracks it forcefully into the wall behind him. Then again, again, Matt is out cold as his blood sprays the wall behind him. Nils fastens his pace, slam after slam. Blood trickling down Matt's face. Nils breathes out, wiping the perspiration from his forehead with his forearm.

As he stands above Matt's corpse, he turns, slowly, to look at where the panel were sat. There, he sees them still. Staring onward, rigid in fear. Nils laughs, properly, with genuine humour.

NILS
Fuck you. FUCK YOU. This is what you crave, isn't it?

He throws his hand to the dead Matt, we see the self-inflicted wound in gory detail.

NILS
This satisfies your quota, right? Don't you see, you're one of them!

Nils laughs again, eyebrows furrowed, eyes glassy. He knows there is no way out to benefit him. He curtsies, dropping low, and long. His eyes drop, mid-curtsy, to the gun - laid on the floor.

NILS
You know. Checkhov said you shouldn't introduce a gun if it isn't fired in the final act.
He stretches his back, toying with the panel. A long, cripplingly tense silence clutches the room.

NILS
Thank you. For the opportunity.

He smirks, shaking his head before leaving through the door.

4. EXT. CITY STREET - **CONTINUOUS**
Nils walks out of the casting room, the dying sun beating on his skin as he smiles. High from the performance of his life, a mix of his and Matt's blood dripping from his hands.

He walks down an alley, beaming. In the out of focus background, a car screeches to a stop - blue lights flashing. Nils carries on walking. We see the door opening, hi-vis police offers. Nils smiles, in his own world.

CREDITS ROLL
END FILM

71

CHANGE - NOT THE LOOSE COINS YOU DENY
HALF DEAD DRIFTERS. NO.
CHANGE THAT SITS IN MY EMPTY STOMACH.
~~LIFE~~ NATURE DEMANDS AGE DEFEATED
"out with the old - in with the new"
AGE PARALYSES DICTATORS + GOVERNMENTS
THAT CLUTCH too MUCH power
for TOO LONG.
LOOK HOW THE HEDONISTS + THE RICH
DEMAND AN UNINTERRUPTED GAZE.
"IN WITH THE OLD - OUT WITH THE NEW."
YOU GET SO FUCKING SICK YOU
DON'T EVEN NOTICE THE
HOMELESS ANYMORE.
YOU SHOOT OUR FINGERS SO WE CAN'T SCRATCH
YOUR ANKLES AND YOU'LL LICK YOUR WOUNDS AND
THE OPPRESSORS TRIUMPH. Fuck the Tories.

INTERVIEWS
Interviews conducted by Nimisha Menon, editor of the Indie Shorts Magazine

GREENLIGHT | interview with actor Jack Parr

NIMISHA: How did you arrive at the story of Greenlight and came to be associated with the series?

JACK: Funny story actually! One day I received an email from a hacker saying they have my password and can access my computer and they've been watching what I've been doing and recording my actions. They put "we've seen *everything*. If you don't send £800 via PayPal we'll release what you don't want to be seen on social media for ALL your family to see."

I mean, my guess was it's a scam – but what if it wasn't? He had my password after all, what if he could access my computer? This scared me quite a lot, I told Gage all about it and we decided to make something out of it. (P.S: Nothing ever happened, I got some professional advice and what they do is get an old password from a weak server you used years ago and hope you are still using the same password to scare you with it") Gage, after the idea, typically goes away and returns within a few weeks with a script. He anxiously waits for a response to see if I like it or not and more than often, I do.

We started working on the script and we were so happy with the result, Gage decided to make more of these 'short films' which very quickly ended up as a mini-series.

NIMISHA: Do you have a better understanding of your characters when you're involved from the very inception of its writing?

JACK: Yes 100%, I think one difficult thing about auditioning for projects, is that we get a couple of sides from our agent and told to audition with absolutely NO idea of who the character is or what he's doing in the film. Which I suppose is part of the magic, they want to see what we come up with. But it's far easier when you've breathed it from the start, you understand the character, their intentions, objectives and why they want what they want, because you've done the journey with them. I do prefer to work on things from the very start.

NIMISHA: How important is spontaneity to you in terms of acting? Or are you the sort who prefers to remain the director's clay to mould?

JACK: A little bit of both but more swaying to the rehearsal and sticking to the script side of things. I do believe if something doesn't feel right or does feel right in the moment you should or shouldn't do it. But going way off script improvisation is not my cup of tea. Mainly because it's a nightmare to edit. If the actors stick to the script and what they've rehearsed, then the edit should (in theory) be a smooth road. If the whole shoot is full of improvisations, I'm guessing the editor has a nightmare of a job.

I write, so I know how much effort and research goes into a script, then you go into rehearsals and flesh it all out and see what works and doesn't and then you go onto set and perform, I agree if something feels right in the moment and it's bloody amazing – *do it*! Apart from that, stick to the darn script.

However, you can stick to the script and the lines – but be spontaneous in the way you perform your lines. That's the art of acting, it's to perform your lines in the most interesting, exciting and engaging way possible.

NIMISHA: Co-stars are often credited with the success of a scene. In Greenlight, although you have only one (Chloe played by Alexandra Marlin), her presence is limited to the phone's screen. What have you learnt from filming for such scenes?

JACK: The *big* difference to acting with a pre-recorded actor on a phone is there's no chemistry. You have to adapt to how the co-actor works on the pre-record. For example, when I'm rehearsing, I could have wanted a bigger gap between her line and mine, but maybe the pre-record didn't allow that so I had to rush a few lines to allow her to speak again, otherwise, we would have overlapped.

It's just about adapting, a lot of directors ask you to do a scene in a totally different way to how you practiced, just to see if you can adapt. I've been asked to do a shockingly evil scene with the intention of flirting, just to see what happens. So, when you step on set, you have to be up for being flexible with your performance. If you're stubborn and want it doing your way, it can mess the whole system up.

NIMISHA: Sam's character is less than idealistic, as are most humans. How important or unimportant is it to you to like the characters you play? Or even to identify with them?

JACK: I'm very good at keeping personal opinions away from characters. I've known actors turn down leading roles because they kiss the same sex right at the end of the film, right at the last minute the character does something the actor doesn't agree with and they're out, it sounded like a great movie too. So, if you don't keep your opinions to yourself you may never work. How can you have a career where you love every single motivation and decision a character makes. I don't think that's possible. But, saying that, I do enjoy connecting with the characters I play and I do love playing characters I like, but I wouldn't turn down a role because they do something I don't agree with – I don't know if you agree but, is that not the role of an actor? To play somebody else.

NIMISHA: For someone whose demeanour is so composed and glamorous, he cracks up quite easily. What did you count on, to get under his skin?

JACK: I find it quite hard to crack like that convincingly. At the time I didn't think I was doing it justice, and even watching it after I wasn't sure some parts were convincing (maybe that's the self-criticism creeping in). But people seemed to believe it, so I would say if you can't find something inside, just go for it anyway and give it 100% effort. We can't sit around all day waiting for an actor to find a certain emotion, sometimes you just have to crack on and get it done.

Although, a lot of that sort of work is done in the prep, what makes you or the character trigger, you have to discover that in rehearsals or in your own prep. Sometimes, what you practiced in prep doesn't work on set, so you have to quickly think of another tactic to get you going. Sometimes nothing works in prep, and then in the moment when the cameras start rolling you just crack and the emotion is flying around your body. I'm guessing some of the top actors can switch it on and off, they must have really learnt how to use their bodies and emotions. I'm not quite there yet. Sometimes it happens and sometimes it doesn't.

The last scene, I really did feel it. Just staring into space, the alarm goes off, I know my whole life ahead of me is going to be a nightmare, years of hard work, and this very moment it will all come crashing down. A single tear rolls down my face. I cheekily say to myself - "You got it Jacky Boy, keeping staring into space" and then I hear cut.

NIMISHA: You embodied Sam so effortlessly. Even sans dialogues, you'd have made him believable. How do you immerse yourself into the characters you play?

JACK: The most important thing I learnt at Drama Classes is you have to make the character human. We all relate to human beings. Many actors fail by acting the part. They over act at everything, it's all a musical. Whereas, if you pick up the phone and chat to your agent, just pick it up and chat don't even think about it. You wouldn't stand there and chat, you'd be doing your laces, rushing to get the bus to work, or making marmite on toast whilst your phone is tightly squeezed into your ear with your shoulder - we are busy humans. You should have learnt your lines so well that you can walk around do your day to day jobs whilst on the phone doing your lines. Because humans don't think when they talk, we've learnt English so bloody well, when our parents call us we can do three different things whilst chatting, so should an actor on set, you shouldn't even be thinking about your lines, you should be thinking what the character is thinking in that scene, and that's normally their next move or a problem they've just faced. So, when I get a script, I really try and just make the character human, what would I do? How would I talk? What would I do in this situation? Because at the end of the day – I'm playing the part. Actors want to get as far away as themselves as possible that it looks unbelievable. The audience wants to see real humans on screen to relate to – not actors.

NIMISHA: The price of fame is different for different people. For some, it's just a loss of privacy. What's the most that you have had to pay so far?

JACK: I haven't experienced fame yet – and I may never experience it. If you become an extremely talented actor it is inevitable that fame is a by-product of your career. So, I think you have to accept it if that's what you want to do. However, what I have experienced is small circle of fans who follow and enjoy my work and write to me and ask for signatures etc. Which is all lovely, I really appreciate people supporting my craft. But the worst things I've experienced so far is people not asking permission to do things. I got asked by an artist if he could draw me. I checked his work out and he draws naked people. I thought, that's not for me, I'm not a still life model. He went ahead and drew me anyway and made up what he couldn't see. That picture will be out in the world that is totally made up. People might think I actually did that. This is another thing you have to put up with, even if you say no, people will go ahead and do it anyway.

NIMISHA: What was the challenging part of playing Sam and what came by easily?

JACK: The challenging parts of playing Sam were getting to the emotions needed. On screen it seemed like such a small thing – he received an email? So what? But to find the emotion that this could potentially end Sam's career was difficult. It was all internal and I was basically alone seeing as my co-worker was in LA when we were filming. So, I had nobody to bounce off, argue with, cry with, I had to do all the work on my own. Some people might thrive on this being left to their own devices, but I struggled.

The easiest part was playing Sam. We are the same age, same accent, both actors (Except he's a child star and I'm not), we looked the same and apart from Sam being gay, we were pretty much the same person. I enjoyed stepping in his shoes.

NIMISHA: For an actor, a star, their image is the ultimate. How willing are you to separate the artist in you from the paraphernalia?

JACK: I'm happy for people to see the real me, because I have nothing to hide. I had a great upbringing and my parents taught me some extremely valuable values in life. But – I'd like my work to shine on and that be what I'm known for. I don't want my personal life to be in the media. I'd like my work to be the forefront of my name.

REDLIGHT | interview with actor Jake Watkins

NIMISHA: What's the first thing you look out for when you hear a script and in your character, in particular?

JAKE: When I first get a script, I read through it with a cuppa a few times to get a feel of the character. Then I start to find any information that is revealed in the script about the character, for example their age, where they're from, things that are solid facts. Then I will start to get a sense of the character's personality by how they respond to certain situations, that can be a big eye opener as to who this person is. Now I have taken all of this information from the script, I can now use it to start working on my backstory.

NIMISHA: Do you research your characters to understand where they're coming from? Or do you simply rely on what the script says? How important is their backstory to you?

JAKE: Personally I like to do as much research as possible to try and fully understand the character, because I find that helps me discover how the character would react to certain things and situations. As Callum is a male escort, I decided to watch a few documentaries on gay escorting, which I found really helped me understand where he is coming from and also why he is doing this. For me, backstory is also extremely important, your past shapes you as a person, so I think it's so crucial to know your characters past. Therefore I spent a lot of time writing down what I think Callum has been through in his life and how it shaped how he sees the world and himself.

NIMISHA: Some prefer dialogue, some don't. As an actor, which one comes easier to you? Performances that involve a lot of dialogue exchange or otherwise?

JAKE: For me, I'm a sucker for a good dialogue scene, I love being able to bounce off the other actors choices and really be in the moment in a scene. But with Redlight, for half of the episode there is no dialogue, so I had to make sure I kept a monologue going on in my head, having a thought process when acting is so important, so I made sure I knew exactly what my character was thinking the whole time.

NIMISHA: The scene where your character discovers the accident, your acting is phenomenal. What do you focus on when you know you have such limited screen time to convince the audience of your emotions?

JAKE: Aw thank you so much first of all, I'm really glad you enjoyed my acting! So in order to convey realistic and believable emotions, I usually focus on the stakes of the situation, so the stakes in this scene are obviously extremely high, so Callum would be all over the place. Before going into the scene, I like to really sit back and put myself in that situation, and think of how I personally would react. I also find that really physicality helps, if I make my body shake and take shallow breaths, it really helps me get into an emotional state, as exhausting as that is!

NIMISHA: While on the set, what helps you stay focused? Or are you the sort who can easily switch on and off between the characters?

JAKE: Anyone who has ever worked with me on set will let you know I like to have a laugh and don't shut up talking. But a few minutes before a take, I will get myself into the right mindset for that particular scene. For example, if it's an emotional scene, I'm able to get myself worked up a few minutes before.

NIMISHA: How much does the make-up, location etc. help you sink into your character?

JAKE: It definitely helps bring the story alive and make it feel more organic. But as for the character, I would say if I've done enough preparation, then I can sink into my character anywhere.

NIMISHA: A lot of Callum's scenes are filmed when he's alone. Be it the scenes shot in the washroom or otherwise. How isolating or challenging do you find that to be?

JAKE: As I mentioned in an earlier answer, I always like to have an inner monologue/ thought process going on in my head. So for me it doesn't feel challenging or isolating at all, I've got my voice yapping in my head the whole time. I will say though, it adds a bit more pressure, all eyes are on you!

NIMISHA: You are an aficionado of horror. Redlight seems right up your alley in that case. What about the film horrified you the most?

JAKE: Well first of all you're absolutely right, slightly obsessed with horror, it seems to be all I have done, maybe I just give off a horrifying vibe? My parents were actually very worried with the amount of horror films I used to watch when I was a kid. The thing that horrified me for most about this episode is Callum's irrational thinking, he really is so freaked out that he ends up making so many bad choices. You just want to shake him and tell him to calm down and think!

NIMISHA: Jimmy's moments are limited, per se. How much did Dan Sheppard contribute to helping you remain rooted in your character despite his limited screentime? And, how important was that to you? Do you think you'd have performed regardless of it?

JAKE: Dan was so amazing to work with, we got on so well on set! For me, having somebody to play opposite with really does help you play the scene, as it makes it feel natural and you can bounce off of each other's acting choices. Although, I do believe if you are confident enough in your character, you can still make it work without having somebody play opposite you. For example, a lot of the time when I have nobody to read in on a self-tape with me, I'll do the scene with my recorded voice saying the other lines, you just have to make do.

NIMISHA: Neither does the character get a closure, nor does the audience. One keeps wondering at the open-ending. Does Callum play at the back of your mind as much as it does for us? Or have you said your goodbyes?

JAKE: All of the characters I have ever played always stick with me, but I try not to get too emotionally attached. There are so many possibilities as to what happened to Callum, and I cannot wait to explore them in season two.

WHITELIGHT | interview with actor Ole Madden

NIMISHA: This was your debut film. What is the one thing you discovered from being present on the set and being filmed?

OLE: I have studied acting since high school however, up until University, the only sort of acting you learn is that for stage performances, so very over the top and expressive. So when I first joined University it was a big change for me, having lessons such as "acting for camera" where you're taught how to act for television. I realised the huge difference, and at first found it quite difficult to still give a believable performance yet naturalistic as I was so used to performing on stage. I soon after joining University was picked up by a workshop group called "The television workshop" which specialise in television acting and improvisation which helped me massively and actually through them was how I got signed by my Agent. The workshop along side classes at University helped me massively adapt to performing on camera, and I think is now the reason I prefer it.

NIMISHA: Your co-stars had different screen presence. While one was restricted to the laptop screen, the other shared the physical space. What difference did you note in your own performance with their physical presence/absence?

OLE: Being at university, I had worked on previous film sets before with fellow classmates, and had done the odd short film with the Television workshop, so I wasn't entirely new to it all. However, working with other professionals, on a piece this deep and controversial was put together a great short film, so soon settled in. So obviously I had more of a connection with the Rochelle (Aubrey) as we spent a lot of time together during filming, and that relationship helped build the relationship of the characters too which worked very well. Definitely spending that time with her, increased our comfortability around one another which I feel was portrayed in the scene. As well as that, I feel the fact I didn't have that connection with Sam (Mitch) but in a similar way to Aubrey worked to our benefit as Aaron never truly meets Mitch, he spends the whole time hiding behind a screen, so not having as stronger connection and comfort with Sam definitely helped build with the realism in my head of the scene.

NIMISHA: Right from the onset, the deception is established and yet we root for him. The credit of that goes to your acting. How did you imbue Arron?

OLE: In my head, I don't see Aaron as a malicious person at all. I just feel he goes the wrong way about a subject he is obviously quite shy about and takes it too far. I never think at any point Aarons intentions are to hurt anyone, but in that, what he does is extremely wrong, it's just his passion to have something he's never had before gets the better of him, and it escalates out of control. You can see the hurt in him when it all goes bad and I feel his timid personality only makes the situation worse as he's too scared and worried to confront anyone about it.

NIMISHA: Chemistry can't be designed or manufactured. There was an effortless one between you and Rochelle Naylor who played Aubrey. Did you have many rehearsals or was this a happy coincidence?

OLE: I think a huge bonus was that we lived together during the shoot, which meant we spent a lot of free time together, whether that was going over lines in our spare time to her introducing me to the twilight series. In spending all that time together we got to know each other and became quite close, and in that I feel came through in our performance together, The banter between the two characters was similar to that which we would have off screen, so it all came together nicely, in a happy coincidence you could say.

NIMISHA: What drew you to playing Arron?

OLE: Well initially I auditioned to Gage using a different script, and it was only after Gage and I met up and had a chat that I heard about Aaron and the potential storyline. I was instantly in love with the whole idea of catfishing but looking at it from the catfish's perspective and what would drive someone to do it, and in hearing some stories from Gage, really got me intrigued into the concept as a whole and why someone would do it. After future meetings we had a good idea of the character and I was really happy to be playing this loving, innocent boy who finds himself in an awful situation and now having done it, am really looking forward still as to where it can go.

NIMISHA: What did you find most interesting or difficult about portraying him? Were the audience's reaction or acceptance of Arron at the forefront of your mind?

OLE: What I found really interesting is how devoted and intrigued he is when typing anonymously to Mitch, and how much he changes in order to try get as much as he can from

Mitch for his own self gain. It's almost a completely different person, from how he is with Aubrey to messaging Mitch at night after waiting up for hours. This almost psychotic behaviour was really interesting for me to look into, and even though he's far from a psychopath, these subtle hints and the lengths he was willing to go to were definitely a fun challenge to try and portray. A huge factor in helping me get into Aarons mind and why he does what he does was hearing other people's own experiences online and why they catfished people. This allowed me to look at the situation from a real catfishes' perspective and then allowed me to in a way sympathise with Aaron. I found that essential before I looked any further with my character development was placing myself in Aarons mind and thinking why he would do it.

NIMISHA: The complexity of the character is in his own mind's dilemma. Do you think Arron would have at any stage outgrown his need to deceptively approach people?

OLE: I don't think Aaron helps himself by putting himself in these types of situations. He is an extremely timid character I feel when it comes to his sexuality and dating hence why he tries to dull it down whenever Aubrey brings it up, and we can tell by her excitement on the subject topic that it's a rare occurrence. In his mind it's the only way he can get his pleasure. However, close calls such as this are definitely a wakeup call and believe would be a big part in his decision to sort of think to himself, I'm not a bad person and I don't want to see the people I love get hurt. On the other hand, this could almost fuel his hunger to try again next time, but harder.

NIMISHA: Was it difficult to let go of Arron once the filming was done? Is it difficult/easy to shirk off the emotions you bring forth for the sake of your character?

OLE: Absolutely, like any performance I feel to give the best performance you must to the best of your ability agree with, believe and become your character. Adopt their thoughts, beliefs and emotions and dropping that just like that is definitely hard and you do miss the character you've been training to become. But that's what the industry in like and I feel as long as you're able to really get into the character you're playing you will always miss them.

NIMISHA: What character and genre would you like to next dabble with?

OLE: I would love to dabble in quite aggressive, passionate, emotional and almost psychotic acting next and look at similar roles and see the difference in prepping for a character like this as exposed to someone like Aaron who is very timid. And as far as genres go I'm not too sure, I think trying as much as possible would be great, as I'd then get to see what I did and didn't like.

STARLIGHT | interview with actor Nathaniel Farah

NIMISHA: Tell us something about yourself and your journey into acting.

NATHANIEL: I've spent a large majority of my life relocating to different countries and cities, having lived in the US and The Netherlands, and the arts, specifically acting, has always allowed me to retain some semblance of familiarity in such unfamiliar places. My sister was the reason I first started acting, due to a primary school teacher suggesting to my parents that she starts a Saturday school for acting to build confidence, and I just wanted to do whatever she was doing. From then on I just continued to join other performing arts classes the older I became until I ended up with a degree in Drama & Performance.

NIMISHA: How did Starlight come into your life?

NATHANIEL: I had applied for a different role in another episode. That role ended up being filled by somebody else, but Gage Oxley, the managing director of Oxygen Films and director of A Series of Light, sent me a message about a role he had in mind for me, I think we spoke for a few hours about the series as a whole, Kane and Jacob and the episode that ended up being Starlight.

NIMISHA: What drew you to Kane? And, what was the most challenging aspect of playing him?

NATHANIEL: How different Kane is to me while sharing a lot of similarities to myself at that age. For example, the confusing exploration of his sexual identity and the way he expresses his emotions. That was also the most challenging part of playing Kane, putting myself back into that mentality of harbouring such shame and anxiety for who you are in a society that is telling you that you are fundamentally wrong.

NIMISHA: The film is set in the 90s. What sort of preparation did it take to get into that headspace? Surely, it isn't about using the right props alone?

NATHANIEL: As Starlight is set in '95 there was a lot of general research into that year and decade as a whole as Kane was 18, as well as a combination of what my / the general mentality was at that age - the naivety, believing you know everything and that you're invincible. Gage and I also had many discussions about the gay culture in the '90s, specifically how Kane would have been impacted by his working-class background in Liverpool, as well as discovering his sexuality during the latter end of the HIV / AIDS epidemic.

NIMISHA: For most films, a lot of the enhancements happen in the post-production, be it the special effects, music, voice-overs, name it. How deeply do you involve yourself with these to understand the narrative style of the film better? Because the very opening scene of Starlight carries with it a dreamy outline that couldn't have been as effective until the post-production.

NATHANIEL: Gage and Faizan Raza, the DoP for Starlight, were so clear with the visions they had for each shot and the visual effects that were going to be done in post. They both also had such great communication with me as an actor, whether it be through their storyboards or just passion for the piece, that I had complete faith that it would turn out beautiful, and it most certainly did.

NIMISHA: The most intimate scene an actor has is with the camera and not his co-actors. How unnerving or convenient was it for you to hold the camera's gaze in one of the most intimate scenes of the film?

NATHANIEL: It was terrifying to have to stare longingly into camera, especially due to the circumstances of the scene! And yes, I would definitely say that the first scene has a different level of intimacy for the audience, as it breaks the fourth wall, although due to the nature of the episode I would have to say that the intimate scenes I did with James Coutsavlis (Jacob) were equally as tense to film. James is such an incredible actor though and the kindest person, so it was a blessing having a friend to act alongside.

NIMISHA: Kane's character is very internalised. With limited dialogues, it's his sporadic outbursts that become his release (referring to the tiff with the kids playing outside and in the climax). How did you understand Kane and what was your process like to embody the character?

NATHANIEL: Music for me has always played such an important part of preparing for a role or creating a piece of work/character. As you said, Kane may not say a lot of dialogue wise but there's lots of noise blaring on in his head, so for me as an actor, creating a playlist of songs that I think Kane would listen to was essential. I also added songs that could place myself into the headspace of what Kane was feeling in a specific scene. I think one song that best encapsulated Kane as a whole throughout Starlight is Iron Sky by Paolo Nutini; a tense ballad that builds to an impassioned monologue.

NIMISHA: Do you get attached to the characters you play? If so, how do you disengage yourself from them?

NATHANIEL: I do, but it depends on the character. For me, when I try to create or develop a character, the process is collaborative, in the sense that I include aspects of myself into that person and adopt parts of them. The process is different for everyone, as of yet that works best for me, maybe it'll change and develop, but the idea of intense method acting and literally "being" somebody else, doesn't work for me.

NIMISHA: What do you want the audience to take away from Starlight?

NATHANIEL: I feel lucky to be able to call Gage Oxley a very close friend of mine, his storytelling is so gritty and unique, we've had hour-long discussions about Starlight and what it means to us as queer people/artists. For me, I view it as a story about unrequited love that can be a very unique experience for many queer people, with roots in a very important time for the LGBTQ+ community, but navigates through universal emotions that everyone can take something from.

NIMISHA: What kind of stories would you like to get associated with in the future?

NATHANIEL: There's always been an underlying fear of mine that I would be pigeonholed into only getting "gay" roles, as I have been turned down the opportunity to audition for someone's film because they didn't believe I could "play straight". I am able to play different types of people, but there is something special about being a part of productions that discusses queer topics, with queer people telling their own stories and experiences.

BLACKLIGHT | interview with actor Charlie Harris (on behalf of Amazon Prime)

LIAM: Tell us something about you, and how you got into acting?

CHARLIE: I use acting as a creative outlet whenever possible because it allows me to step away from the monotony of every day life and slip into another persons. I started loving acting at about 8 at school. My first role was a boxer in Bugsy Malone. I'll never forget that feeling of being up on stage and waiting for the audience's reaction, meanwhile they have no idea that you're terrified and about to pass out! But that's where the excitement comes from.

LIAM: How involved were you with crafting Adam, and Blacklight as a whole?

CHARLIE: The writer and director Gage and I have been in contact for years. We always knew we worked well together so from the very first mention of the story he had we began to collaborate. Adam is (obviously) a terrible person. Gage and I have come into contact with many people who are potentially like him behind closed doors which definitely helped us with the direction of where he was going. He was a really fun character to mould and adapt, we didn't have too many redirections with him because we both had a clear image of what he should be from early on.

LIAM: Adam is a spectacularly vile, yet clearly vulnerable, character to have to breathe life into. Do you research the character to understand where they're coming from? How important is their backstory to you?

CHARLIE: Adam has human qualities in him somewhere, they just don't know how to manifest. The idea we wanted to portray with him was that he's very confused. The best way to research individuals like this is to go on forums and certain chat sites. The internet breeds self doubt and narcissism all in one. It lets you be as confident and arrogant as you like, but then when you see someone being similarly bullish or rude, you are taken a back. This, I feel, is all Adam has done for years. Very little human contact but plenty of internet does not help the brain. I needed this research to help me understand the characters motivations towards even his own family.

LIAM: There are some very poignant and beautifully shot moments which in essence are quite shocking. What was the most challenging aspect of playing Adam?

CHARLIE: The set was amazing. The professionalism and talent on that set was incredible. The scene where Adam stands up in front of the mirror agonisingly staring at himself was demanding in terms of me recognising that Adam and I share similar insecurities just to varying degrees.

INTERVIEWS

LIAM: Adam has a lot of alone time in the film. Did you find so much isolation as an actor help or hinder your character when you have no one to act off of?

CHARLIE: I found acting alone to be refreshing. I like acting with someone but for this film that narrative just didn't fit the mood. The fact that Adam spends so much time alone in his day means that he must be comfortable with it. Spending time alone in real life is the only thing to prepare you for a role like this.

LIAM: Adam represents a growing movement of men who are seemingly underground, but Blacklight presents them very visibly within the community. Do you think it's important to portray such characters?

CHARLIE: I think the more it's talked about then the more coverage we bring to it. It might seem easier to ignore these people on the internet and dismiss them as just another sub culture. But that's too easy because they are already feeling cast aside by the rest of the world; the best way to help is by bringing peoples attention to it and being aware of it.

LIAM: Blacklight is full of very memorable scenes, but one which enthrals the viewer is right at the beginning of the film. How important was Gage's presence as a director to achieving that scene?

CHARLIE: Yeah the first one seemed very 'no shying away' and up front. Again, the professionalism was unmatched on set. We had our first day on set prepping and blocking scene 1. This was my first project in a while and so it relieved me that we had a day to prepare for it, and I feel you can tell we had time to prepare for it as it went so smooth! I really appreciate the thought of easing into such an uncomfortable scene, and I've only got Gage and the crew to thank for that.

LIAM: The ending of Blacklight is purposefully quite ambigious, in that we as a viewer don't really get closure at the same time neither does Adam. Do you think about Adam as much as we do? Or, have you exorcised that demon?

CHARLIE: I feel like I can distance myself from Adam as a character that I've played, but I can't let go of what I've learnt through him. It doesn't weigh my mind down when I think of it but the circumstances behind him are very dark so they are heavy thoughts. But I can't let go of him fully because of SEASON 2! Sorry to wedge that in there but it's exciting and you've got even more in store for the next one, believe me!

LIAM: What do you want the audience to take away from Blacklight?

CHARLIE: This is an interesting question because I still don't know myself! I think the main direction I'd like the film to push them in is that these people look normal, have real human lives and jobs and all of that stuff, but they are so shrouded in mystery that they may never say anything to you in person but torture you from afar. I hope we've conveyed that anyway.

LIAM: What character would you love to play next? Do you have any genres you're keen to tackle?

CHARLIE: I have no preference at all for genre! I'd love to try comedy or romance although it really doesn't matter to me, as long as a role challenges me then that's all I'm after.

LIMELIGHT | interview with actor Bruce Herbelin-Earle (from Viddy Well)

AARON HAUGHTON: How did you hear about Oxygen Films and get involved in this project?

BRUCE: Gage came to me with a script he was excited to talk to me about, we arranged to meet in London for a readthrough and a catchup, and he explained that it was inspired by his despair with current events, political and social - and wanted to combine the two within an industry that he knew all too well about...

AARON: What resonated with you most about the script?

BRUCE: I think the rawness in how Gage wanted to shoot the project was enough to agree to do it. His idea to shoot the monologue in a quiet, still, long continuous take, excited me. In earlier drafts, my character is ignited by a conversation with his girlfriend/partner, but I had trouble creating the high stakes that my character needed to go back into that audition room with a gun - I suggested a mad idea that he could receive a call from his mother, essentially telling him that she'd be stopping his funds because she'd had enough of him. (the idea that she could be French came swiftly after Gage and I started to develop the scene)

AARON: How did you prepare for the role and develop your character?

BRUCE: Lots and lots of rehearsing within the four walls of my bedroom, unfortunately! In the early stages I'd set up a tripod and started to record b-roll on my phone. While watching it back - sometimes I'd find nuances and mannerisms that I liked. The hard work came when Gage and I figured out areas in the script where the tension escalated and whether I wanted to play those moments still and psychotic, or loud and proud. I'm keen on keeping things basic when it comes to pinpointing beats within a scene. I try not to overthink things and like to play around when I get on set to see if I can draw anything more out of the "moment". At the end of the day, Nils is an actor who's desperate for break - I think a few of us know what that can be like... He just happens to go a little further than I think most of us would.

AARON: Are there any fun or humorous tales from the set that you can tell us?

BRUCE: The shoot was many months ago so it's hard to remember anything in particular, but I'm sure Gage has some behind the scene footage somewhere and I'd love to see it.

AARON: What drew you to the performative arts? How did you fall in love with acting?

BRUCE: In the beginning, way back in the days of school performances, it was the opposite of anything "academic" and relied more on self-expression and confidence. Performing Arts class was an escape from Maths, English, and Science. There weren't any guidelines and, as students, we were encouraged that there was no "right way" of doing things - a lesson that I'm constantly reminding myself to this day. I remember playing one of the ugly sisters in my year 5 performance of "Cinderella" and just remember hearing the audience howling at two 10 year old kids in a dress, wig and heels, clip-clopping down the aisle, shouting "CINDERS!! WHERE ARE YOU CINDERS!!"

The feeling of being able to create a reaction like that in front of an audience of around 100+ people was certainly eye-opening. Also, the fact that I was greeted with nothing but smiles and handshakes from parents that I didn't know post-show went a long way to boosting some early needed confidence. You can imagine that this was a pretty big thing to go through as a 10-year-old kid. I was congratulated for being a clown, and it was after THAT performance, that I had been bitten by the "bug", how cliche...

AARON: What are some tips you give those aspiring actors out there for how they can hone their craft?

BRUCE: There are books written by the great masters of acting, read them. Then decide for yourself the kind of actor you want to be by taking snippets of what you learn from each of them. Mel Churcher, Stella Adler, Larry Moss, Patrick Tucker; have all written books based off their experiences in the industry. Many of them give you the do's and don'ts. Take what you want from these books and apply their techniques into your acting.

AARON: Do you have any upcoming projects you can share with us?

BRUCE: I have a few things coming up at the end of the year which I am looking forward too, none of which I am allowed to speak about! Eurgh, annoying isn't it!

A SERIES OF LIGHT | interview with creator Gage Oxley (from Viddy Well)

AARON HAUGHTON: How did you come up with the concept for this series or short films?

GAGE: The concept originated from a conversation with Jack Parr (Greenlight) and Bruce Herbelin-Earle (Limelight), where Jack had received an email from a scammer saying that his webcam had been hacked, and they had video of him masturbating, as well as sending his current password. That initially terrifying moment of being extorted to ensure it isn't sent to friends, family and colleagues dissipated - but the story remained and turned into what the first episode in the anthology explores. What then transpired was the realisation that we could tell a host of unique, different stories mostly in one room, with one or two actors. While it was born from mostly budget constraints, the restriction presented themes of isolation, claustrophobia and modern relationships through technology; merging with narratives which I was really excited to present for the first time.

AARON: The series focuses heavily on the theme of identity, hiding it, revealing it, or discovering it. What do you find most fascinating about this theme?

GAGE: I think the fascinating element of identity is that while everyone has one, our perception is completely unique. What I think about my identity is vastly different to what my closest friends will see, which is again different to what my family or colleagues see. Identity is something so personal and intimate, yet we are living in an age where it's splashed across the internet, dictating our love lives through a swipe, or being the crux in how many likes we achieve. I think identity is becoming something so manipulated and crafted that we lose that sense of freedom; and so that is how *A Series of Light* presents it - identity behind closed doors and four walls. On a more personal note, growing up queer from a council estate in the North of England, I didn't really see my identity around me. Hiding it for years was really very damaging, and I think that queer experience is something that is rarely presented in this format.

AARON: Since you wrote and directed each piece, I'm sure all the stories in the anthology are near and dear to your heart, but I'm curious, do you have a favorite out of the bunch?

GAGE: Ooh - now that is a tough one! Each episode really does have a special place in my heart for very different reasons. With the series being shot across different months, to me it represents a sort of nostalgia and history. The opportunity each episode presented to work with the best people, and collaborate with incredible talent in new and exciting challenges is exactly why I do what I do. Though, if I had to chose, Starlight is the type of film that I would have loved to have seen growing up. It's a really personal, heart-aching story, and Nathaniel Farah (Kane in Starlight) embodies that piercing queer coming-of-age so beautifully.

AARON: Music plays a big part in each film. What did you look for in the backing tracks? Were there any you wrote or structured stories around?

GAGE: I think music is such a massive element of film, and I'm so pleased with how a lot of the tracks are used to evoke response and reaction. Songs like "People Are Strange" which opens Blacklight is incredibly provocative and throws a whole new spin on what would be a really disturbing, explicit entry into the episode. Many of the songs in the film were placed within the script at its writing phase, but there were a handful which were changed in post-production. I remember sitting with our brilliant editor, Thomas J. Harkness and assistant director, Harley Mathews scouring Spotify trying to find the perfect fit for some of the parts of the film which required scoring. My favourite moment of this is when we were editing Greenlight, there was a radio in Sticks and Glass (our post-production house) which was playing "Be My Baby". I remember thinking 'that would be such a better song for the end than the one we have planned', and we got the rights, made the change and sent it off!

AARON: How did you work with cinematographers Rose McLaughlin and Faizan Raza to discover the look for the series?

GAGE: Rose and Faizan are two incredibly talented visionaries and creators. Placing that trust in them to deliver the style and tone for their episodes was so easy because they totally understood the emotion and story we were presenting. Rose, who was the director of photography for Redlight, Whitelight, Blacklight and Limelight, jumps straight into the scene with acute precision and planning - but by shooting handheld allows the camera to be perceived as a character within the film itself. Doing this often shortcuts our connection to the characters, which is especially important where the episodes are so short.

Faizan, who did cinematography for Starlight, achieved such a stylistic representation of the 90s, and his more static, fluid set-ups allowed us to experience the slow burn of the two main characters' desire for one another over a period of several months.

AARON: How did you find your wonderful cast?

GAGE: I've been lucky enough to have worked with a few of our leads over the past few years; I've known and worked with Jack for six years now, so that trust is definitely there. The same goes for Bruce and Samuel Curry (Whitelight) who I've been friends with for a few years since we worked together on another film. I went to college with Charlie Harris (Blacklight) and we studied acting together back in 2014, but what has been exciting is meeting and having the chance to work with so many new and ridiculously talented people. We often put casting calls out through social media, as well as on casting sites such as Mandy; as well as going direct through agencies and universities. I've been really lucky to be able to work with such a brilliantly creative cast who are totally up for the challenges, and open to crafting the stories together.

AARON: I know Oxygen Films is entirely non-profit and self-funded, but can you tell me more about the production company?

GAGE: I set Oxygen up just over five years ago now, mostly due to the fact that as a 17-year-old boy desperate to be in the film industry, I couldn't get any on-set experience due to my age. Then, when I turned 18, suddenly it seemed I couldn't get on set due to lack of experience. This catch-22 felt so infuriating, and so I decided to take matters into my own hands, at first working with school friends and slowly assembling an incredible cohort of young people who are passionate about film, as well as the narratives we produce. Everyone on the team volunteers their time and talent, including cast and crew, with everyone being under the age of 25. We offer a foot in the door to an industry which is difficult at the best of times, but can be remarkably intimidating to any young person from a minority or disadvantaged background. I'm so proud to do what I do, not only because of the direct change our films make, but also to the offer we provide to every person we work with. Now I am very privileged to work with a whole host of people, including our Head of Production, Sian Carry, and our Head of Programmes, Eleanor Hodson, who both worked tremendously hard to get this series out of the door.

AARON: What drew you to the visual arts? How did you get into directing?

GAGE: I've wanted to be a director since I was eight years old. I vividly remember getting a tape camcorder and running around gardens, woods and anywhere else I could find to tell some ridiculous stories. I have a folder of hand-written scripts about aliens, pirates and zombies - and remain quite envious of the imagination my younger self had. My mum took me to see Roberto Benigni's *La Vita é Bella* when I was younger. It was the first subtitled film I remember watching, and it was the first time I recall having such an immense reaction to a film. It was then I realised that that is all I wanted to do for someone else. If I could present a fraction of the way that film made me feel, I would be happy. So from there, I self-taught how to edit, I became involved in my local film festivals, I saved up over Birthdays and Christmas to assemble equipment - and watched, read and engaged as much as I possibly could. I've never wanted to be anything but a filmmaker, and cannot see myself doing anything else.

AARON: What films or filmmakers inspired this series or your overall approach to storytelling?

GAGE: With *A Series of Light* presenting such a diverse range of stories and styles, there is quite a mix of films and filmmakers which inspired me. One name that does keep popping up is David Fincher, whose visual storytelling is stupendous. Lynne Ramsay is another voice who I adore - her representation of violence and the darker aspects of life are so sensitively handled. A personal inspiration is Xavier Dolan whose queer presentations were, and remain, so important to me. While working on a second season, these names, as well as Gasper Noe, are firmly keeping me motivated. In terms of content, I would have to say it has been more television or VOD shows which have inspired me with *A Series of Light*. Stories such as *Fleabag* and *Killing Eve* are a masterclass in dialogue and realism, contrasting with the vibrant distortions and vivid style of *Euphoria*. For me, television is pushing so many boundaries cinematically that I do hope film starts to do.

AARON: What advice would you give to those young filmmakers out there?

GAGE: My advice is to persist. This industry can be a real challenge, and it can take a lot of effort to just continue. If you're working a job on the side, it's being strict in keeping motivated to be creative outside of that. No one is going to make you be proactive, so you have to achieve that yourself. If you want to make a film, then find a camera or borrow a phone. Stay true to who you are, and your voice - try not to let anyone silence that - eventually people will listen.

AARON: What do you hope audiences take away from the film?

GAGE: I hope audiences take away a new perspective of queer life, recognising that LGBTQ* people are not a group, we are individuals with very unique stories and beliefs. I'd love for people to see themselves somewhat represented across the series, all I ever want is for a younger me to feel proud and be able to see some form of them presented on screen, unapologetically.

AARON: Do you have any future projects in the works that you can share with us?

GAGE: Yes! I am working on a second season for *A Series of Light*, which continues the narratives from its first season in the exact same order, some minutes or months later. I'm beyond thrilled to be able to work with this talented cast again, as well as continuing to push boundaries and break cinematic ground as we (hopefully) enter a new artistic renaissance after the lockdown.

STOP GHOSTING ME

As part of "Blacklight", producers needed several paperback book copies of Alexia Ford's critically acclaimed debut novel: STOP GHOSTING ME. Rather than printing blank pages, the production team wrote a dedicated novella which was printed throughout the fifteen limited edition book props the team had printed. In fact, to try and curb costs, the book was (and still is at the time of writing) made available to purchase on Amazon Prime.

The book explores the familiar story of Starlight, presented in a more narrative format.

one

the faint echoes of aching breath ruptured the cold walls of the shared dormitory where kane lay atop crisp sheets. tonight, however, the dorm was empty of anyone else. he was alone with his thoughts, a dangerous thing for a young man like kane.

he was in his first year of university, the first time he had tasted the freedom of his own space and yet it was marred by the presence of another. a boy who too felt the comforting arms of his parents freeing their grasp, his roommate, jacob.

jacob was probably in the lockout at the 051 . he would be gone a while. kane could traverse his own mount pleasant.

a soft hand broke upward between kane's lungs. further and further it danced, circling his bulging adam's apple and tracing his jawline. his fingertips crawled across his right cheekbone, venturing the contour leaning down to bitten lips.

his free hand slumbered beyond his abdomen, embracing himself, as if no one else yet had. kane's eyes shut, the corners of his brows pulled down. this solitary moment was for him alone.

of course, it wasn't long before the rogue arm slipped below the grey fabric hem of his underwear. a subtle change in his steady exhalation registers kane's desire for touch. though, after a few longing strokes, an unwelcome vision attacked kane. no . he thought. he rejected it.

but another came, dancing across his synapses and seeping into lucid vision with vivid colours. he no longer could deny himself. he saw it. he wanted to see it.

carefully kane mustered another slip of his wrist, a hum from the back of his throat escaped into the room. he hadn't done this for a while. the last month had been rocky. with jacob metres away from him he could hardly do anything. plus the bathroom was shared by the entire corridor and he wasn't- one more image. longer and harsher. kane winced. it was actually starting to hurt him.

fuck off . he thought.

his back cracked as he arced above the mattress. the feathered pillows depressing and wheezing a cosy crash. his stomach dipped, he was close.

kane's pace grew quicker. as did his breathing. his tongue stretching below his gritted teeth as the celestial burst loomed in the pit of his iliac furrow. but a third vision krept and took hold. the worst of them all. his dry mouth retaliated.

he couldn't think about it for long. the door flew open, spilling in the hallway light which licked the walls as kane gathered his bedsheets and turned, praying he hadn't been caught.

then he heard him. *shh shhh* . it was jacob. *he's sleeping* . followed by the unmistakeable noise of fabric hitting the floor and bodies hitting the bed. they giggled and kissed. *oh shit*. jacob moaned.

fuck . he thought.

two

stephanie seymour slapped the table. she was an ace. michael threw her down. then anna nicole smith, a king, by kane. *ah she's me favourite* . leered michael. *what about elle macpherson?* posed jacob. *who?* said michael. *this one* . smiled jacob as he chucked a queen on the pile.

fuck mate i'd bend her over this table . michael sniffed. *yeah, like you'd have a chance with your hands in your trackies* thought kane, but instead he smirked. *you wanna ciggy?* asked michael as he stretched the pack to jacob, who nodded and slipped one from the box. *bet you'd love a fag though ey* . winked michael. kane broke from the game. it was directed at him. his stomach twisted. *fuck off* . he laughed. but he took one.

it was jacobs turn. he was taking too long. staring at the cards as the cig dropped from his lips. he looked a bit like james dean. in that rogue, good boy gone bad way. then he dropped an eight. *you got your dick wet yet mate?* slithered michael as he played another eight. *yeah mate. steph and jen. they left walkin' funny didn't they kane?* jacob's eyes glinted as he clocked kane's. smug prick kane thought. *thought they was gettin' killed the way they screamed like* . kane hoped he was off the hook, but michael kept on. *you get any of jakey boy's sloppy seconds?* kane threw in a five. *nah. i can catch me own-* kane began. *-and out.* jacob finished.

michael twisted his neck round to jacob. *how in the fuck you lucky prick?* jacob laughed. kane smiled, dropping his eyes to his remaining deck. *thank fuck for that* . kane mused silently. as he collected the array of attractive women in lingerie, others without, that plastered the playboy cards, kane felt unmistakably present. a feeling he hadn't experienced growing up in toxteth, a council estate of block terraced houses cramped together. he grew up on isaac street, learning which house the drug dealer lived at by the age of six. he didn't really know what a drug dealer was. but he knew he was a friend of da's.

another? kane eyed jacob who nodded. *listen i'm gonna get off.* michael sighed, one of the arms breaking from inside his grey joggers and up to his snorting nose. *already?* kane began. then thought how he would prefer the company of just jacob and stopped. *got things to do 'ant a lad* . The corner of michael's lips raised. kane knew better than to ask what errands he'd be running, but jacob cut in anyway. *lookin' for your da again are you?*

the room plummeted. the white noise sliced the breath from kane. michael's tongue lingered. *what have you just said?* he wanted to hear it again. jacob looked up from rifling the playing cards. he laughed. *what?* jacob grinned. *it was nothin'. jus' a joke.*

a joke? just a joke? you're a fuckin' joke. michael spat, upper lip curling in venom. *mikey. calm down.* kane's gut lurched. why had he joined the fray? *don't you fucking tell me to calm down.* michael raged, then twisted back to jacob. *you know nuttin' about me an' me family.* jacob raised his hands staring deep at michael. all that remained between them was the cigarette smoke and a healthy dose of tension.

fuckin' prick. michael jumped from his chair and round, opening the door and slamming it behind him. jacob collapsed the cards in his hands onto the table. kane followed. he stared at jacob, at least he'd got what he wanted.

three

what the fuck even is he? jacob slurred. kane looked at the clock. it's only 2pm and you're already high and drunk. kane wondered how jacob was in university at all. he looks like a right nonce. continued jacob. kane eyed the television set, propped precariously by an array of vhs's and books. on the screen was the wobbling mr blobby of noel's house party.

kane returned to his work, the corner of his mouth twitching as he attempted to mask his smile. jacob lolled off his bed and arced over the television set. moments later, muffled moans and soft brassy music emitted from the tv. jacob dropped his shorts and jumped onto the bed.

from the peripherals of his eyes, kane glimpsed jacob as he toyed with the snaking bulge of his white briefs. *what the fuck is he doing?* kane screamed silently. then, jacob cleared his throat, ending it with a soft groan. kane buried his paperwork deeper into his lap, masking his own stir. jacob's hand was now gripped within his underwear. kane's eyes were drawn in front, a desperate look before darting to the television. *he's wanking over the spice network.* kane swallowed his judgment. *i've got... um... porn?* kane stuttered.

jacob carried on masturbating, glassy eyes lay fixated on the screen. *yeah. sure.* he breathed quietly, voice low and aching.

kane gave it a moment before placing his paperwork on the bed and kneeling down to the television. he pulled out a vhs from the side of the messy collection. ghost to ghost. it was relatively new. kane hadn't seen it yet. he'd bought it when he was only seventeen in an adult store. they had asked for his id, and when he passed his provisional with shaking hands the shop owner just smiled and said *it's still a tenner. we don't do student discount* . the vhs slotted into the tv and within a few seconds, the grey static rolled and the picture started. it was an advert. a naked woman laid across an armchair with a telephone. below was a number to call to speak to her. kane couldn't think of anything worse.

jacob's hand was now gripping outside his underwear, hand massaging his hard penis which curved to the right brief leg. he had moved over the bed, offering a space for kane to join him.

kane's heart beat propelled in his chest like a trapped bird in a cage. he sat beside jacob, immediately feeling the warmth of his body close beside him. *this is too much* . kane told himself. but his arm operated subconsciously, fingertips unfastening the stud at the top of his trousers. left hand extending into his own boxers too. his gaze burnt the television, fighting the urge to look to his left and see jacob in the throes of self-pleasure. he managed to get away with a couple of quick glances.

then, jacob slowly pulled his hand away from his stroking, and glided toward kane, skirting over his abdomen and battling the tight free space in his underwear to grip his member. kane gasped. eyes racing, from jacob who remained staring ahead to his hand that trailed kane's erection.

kane momentarily bolted his thoughts back together and slinked his arm below jacob's and down into his friend's boxers. kane felt the warmth in his hand. a million arrows pierced his skull as he was pelted with every thought.

what if i'm doing it wrong. what if i get too hard. what if i cum. why is he doing this. is he wanting this too. what if he's not enjoying this.

but it was broken by a soft moan slipping from jacob as he craned his neck back. kane too was breathing heavier, watching his hand fall up and down in jacob's briefs. kane's pace quickened, desperate to give jacob even a fraction of the pleasure he was feeling right now. jacob reciprocated his speed, thumb flicking the head of kane's penis. kane sighed, eyes rolling in ecstasy, then falling back down to jacob. the flickering colours of ghost to ghost fell upon jacob as if the god's were illuminating him.

kane was desperate to gather the space between them, so he shifted slightly into the gap. then a little more. jacob was moaning more frequently. kane moved his gaze from jacob's groin up his stomach and onto his face. he leaned into jacob. who turned and retreated quickly. *what the fuck?!* protested jacob. he shot up and away, off of the bed. adjusting himself in his briefs and hurriedly pulling up his shorts. kane remained transfixed forwards as the subtle grunts and slaps of the video continued. jacob was already out of the door.

four

the two boys walked down a tree-lined street in quiet slumber, swamped in april rainwater. the dull hit of a ball scattering the asphalt skimmed in front of them. kane spotted them first. a young boy, who looked no older than ten, and wearing a yellow arsenal top that was at least three sizes too big for him. he kicked the ball to another boy, older, around fifteen. he wore a manchester united shirt. he kicked it back to the younger boy who stumbled with the ball and sent it rolling to the feet of kane.

why you kickin' an arsenal footie for? kane couldn't hide his disgust as he interrogated the younger boy. the older boy, his brother as it would turn out, interjected. *why you talking to a twelve year old, you nonce.* jacob had carried on walking but stopped to turn back to kane, who kissed his teeth at the older boy. *kick it back then you poof.* crowed the older lad. kane smiled, turned, and blasted the football down the opposite way of the boys. *eh what you done that for?* whined the younger boy as he ran after the ball. his brother followed, cutting between kane and jacob. as he passed, he turned and spat on the floor.

kane carried on down the path, jacob a few steps behind as he watched the young boy collect his ball. he ran after kane, laughing. *you feel better now, yeah?* he elbowed kane. *they fuckin' deserved it* . kane argued. he was relieved jacob was talking to him again. the past few days since their mutual masturbation had been trying. *did you see that little twat's face when you kicked his ball. what the fuck was he wearin' an' all. looked like a dress an' the colour of piss.*

kane laughed, the gentle breeze taking hold of their light conversation as they wandered the path.

five

kane was once again alone in the dorm. jacob was out somewhere. he'd been out somewhere for the past thirteen nights. kane had stopped asking where he was going after the fifth.

a tab of lsd rested on kane's forefinger. it had the red inkings of a loveheart dashed on the blot. kane looked at it. he'd always wanted to try it but had never taken the plunge. i'm going to do it he told himself. i really am . but he'd been staring at the empty bed opposite him for nearly forty minutes now.

how can something this small have a big effect? kane reasoned. promptly snapping the quarter inch paper on his tongue.

m o o n l i g h t w a s h e s o v e r h i m a s k a n e l a y s w i t h h i s b a c k a g a i n s t j a c o b s b e d.

he feels the burning amber from the sodium lights outside their window resting upon him, sinking into his features. kane leans back, head rolling, desperate for a view outside these four lonely walls.

~~but the~~ k a n e f o u n d h i m s e l f o u t s i d e . e v e n t h o u g h i t w a s m a y, a n d t h e n i g h t s h a d
d r a w n c o l d e r, k a n e w o r e o n l y a b l a c k t e e.

euphoria plastered his face, the streetlamps glow and glisten, a sparkle dripping over kane as he danced and wanders through the estate. the dark draping sky is filled with vibrant colours. hues of pinks, purples and fiery gold which twinkle and burst. the fireworks bellow and blast, rocketing the stage in front of kane. a hand grips his. kane looks. jacob.

~~i fucking love him but i can't have him.~~
w h y n o t ? i d e s e r v e h i m.

kane looked up at the clear stars, mapped in astral light, flinging themselves upon him as he craned his neck, desperate to be among the divinity.

on his feet, as they traverse the bulging cobbles, drenched in pools of may rainwater. his outstretched face, now with starlight tearing below his eyes in elysian beauty. he comes down, feet back firmly on the ground, as he looks around. kane glides through the street, stacked terraces either side as he pushes the universe backwards.

~~starlight~~

walk

~~i am five. hi mum.~~

keep walking

~~starlight~~

keep fucking walking

~~men fucking~~

don't look

~~i hate this place~~

get out

~~jacob grinding dick fuck~~

stop it

~~da shouting. i'm hurting please don't~~

this is your own fault

~~i fucking want jacob. i want him~~

don't

i want jacob.

six

june was hot. too hot. it was towards the end of the month, and the entirety of liverpool had realised the only way to be moderately cool was to wear as little as possible.

three oscillating fans billowed air around the stuffy dorm, paper streamers waving from the metal corrugation. *it's just blowing hot air at us you know.* kane complained.

jacob ignored him. slamming his thumbs on the control pad of the sega in front of them. jacob had acquired the fans. kane had suggested the sega. both of them had silently agreed to wear boxers. the sweat stuck to their bodies as jacob lurched his body, cracking the controller. *stop button mashing! yo you're cheatin' mate.* jacob knelt up, eyes glued to the blue glow. *check out this fatality!* more crashing of buttons and sticks and kane drops his controller. jacob smiled. *another round?* kane sighed. he laid on the floor beside jacob who remains knelt up. you need to get on my level first. jacob's voice drawled. amongst the scent of the boy's sweat is the unmistakable stench of cannabis. *you only beat me because you're fuckin' spaced out your mind.* kane retorted, laughing. *exactly. eat acid. smack you with sub zero.*

silence took over the room, the slow whir of the fans holding the conversation. *it's so fucking hot.* kane groaned. more silence. jacob clicked through the menu, setting the next game up. but he stopped. a moment's thought.

have you ever got off wi' a lad?

kane's heart pounded. *fuck.* how could he answer that. he'd waited too long to say it. *no*. he said. but it's the wrong thing isn't it. kane's mind raced. a celestial explosion behind glazed eyes. the fans ache and stutter. the television goes dark. *shit.* jacob sighs, *leccy's gone.* he threw the controller on the floor.

another moment in silent hesitation. listen . jacob played with his hands in front of him. kane remained outstretched on the floor. *when we was wankin'* jacob trailed off then. *why'd you... y'know?* kane knew. *i think-* kane needed to plan his words. *i don't know. i guess i wanted to. to know what it felt like.* jacob picked his fingernails. *are you a homo?* jacob asked. he wasn't entirely sure he wanted the answer. but it was too late by then. there was no answer for some time. jacob glanced at kane - *no* - he blurted immediately.

kane sits up now, returning to jacob's level. *well, i don't think so. i've never kissed a lad before. that's why. and... we was messin' around... i don't know. i just thought-*

kane's spiralling confession was cut short by jacob who had pushed into him, kissing him tentatively. they broke apart for a second, for kane it felt like a life time. then, kane was pushed back onto the floor as jacob lifted a leg over him, sitting above kane's torso - pinning his arms down. jacob stared at a breathless kane. jacob's face was full of frenzied desire. he was an intimidating force. jacob leaned over to the bed beside him, picking up a rolled joint and lighting it. He toked on it once, exhaling a cloud of deep smoke. then, slithering down kane's body. jacob pulled kane's boxers down, taking him in his mouth.

seven

jacob woke first. the dorm which, just hours earlier had been filled with searing oranges and reds of the june sun now a cool english night. still, jacob could still feel kane's perspiration beside him. their bodies entangled, arms below heads, legs over and under each other.

jacob lifted kane's head and rolled him over, releasing himself. he sat up. immediately feeling a wetness on his abdomen. he looked down and dragged his finger across a collection of cum on his stomach, wiping it on a pair of boxers beside him.

fuck he whispered.

he trivially ground a bud of marijuana, tipping it into some rolling paper, liberally sprinkling tobacco over it. as he rolled the spliff, he was drawn to the sleeping boy beside him. he shut his eyes. hoping, desperately, that if he couldn't see his shame he wouldn't feel it.
flick. the flame sizzled as he lit the joint between his lips.

i would say i loved you

                but saying out loud is hard

so i won't say it at all.

           and i won't stay very long.

      i do

           love you.

              i do

                  love you.

          but words are futile devices

eight

july is when kane left. he was there one day and gone the next. the last few items had only just been packed away when jacob returned. *shit. you leavin' now?* he sounded surprised. but he knew this day was coming. *back to me da's. then...* kane trailed off. the worst thing was he hadn't had a plan. no idea where his life was taking him.

yer could always stick around like. i mean, it's been good, mate. you're a sound lad an'... i dunno.

kane could physically feel his heart tearing into two. aching pulses rippling his body. *it's been good? it's been good? tha's it is it? fuck me.* kane shook his head, retreating to his boxes beside him. jacob's face fell, then. *what the fuck else am i meant to say, eh?* jacob stepped closer to kane. fury bubbled up within him. *you want me to say how much i liked seein' you spaff over me, is that it?* jacob's featured contorted, twisting hard and sharp below the harsh daylight.

fuck off jacob. kane muttered, looking up at jacob from his scrawling 'kane' on the front of the box. *or... the kick i got fuckin' you like a fag?* jacob spat vitriol, disgust. at kane. or himself. kane snapped, standing. *i said fuck off!* kane slammed his closed fist quickly into jacob's face. colliding with his nose. jacob's head cracked backwards. blood fell from jacob's nostrils, over his lips. they are silent.

jacob stepped towards kane. his knuckles stinging. another step closing the gap. then. jacob kissed kane. kane struggled to wriggle free.

you're fucking mental, mate. you high now, yeah? 'cos that's the only time you'd ever do owt. kane's voice trembled, hands flying up to his head, fingers sifting through his hair. *fuck sake. you wreck me head, like.*

kane collapsed onto his bed. jacob stood still by the door, his cold face void of emotion.

i feel fuckin' sick. an' i get it. i get why you have to have a spliff or... whatever. 'cos if you felt anythin' like i do, i'd want to be fuckin' numb. so i do get it like. but i can't keep doin' this.

kane breathed, then. swallowing his hurt. *i'm not that lad.* he finished.

jacob exhaled. looked round the room. god, it's empty.

i'm not that lad either. maybe that's the problem. jacob breathed through his nose, shakey inhalations. he probably didn't mean it to come out as cutting as it had. but it had sliced kane already and he could tell. the silence was deafening. though, interrupted by a car horn. the two looked around, to the window.

tha's me da. kane noted. he didn't want it to end like this. he didn't really want it to end at all. if... *if you ever become that lad. find me. won't you.*

jacob scratched his head. one last look around. he opened the door for kane.

yer da's waiting.

he couldn't keep eye contact with kane. kane nodded. he understood. with a box in his hands, he left through the open doorway. jacob grabbed one of kane's boxes and followed, only a step behind him.

SECOND LIGHT

As I put together this book in the Summer of 2020, quarantined and desperate to be back on set, or at least with Human contact, the one silver lining is that I have been able to meet and collaborate with some absolutely incredible talent in producing a second season of A SERIES OF LIGHT.

Due to go into production towards the end of this year/start of 2021, producers, co-writers and our prodigious talent are crafting new, provocative and important narratives to bring to life. The revolutionary second season will be a direct sequel of the first, in the same order, with narratives continuing minutes, months or years after. The series is produced by Sian Carry, Eleanor Hodson and myself.

Not only do I get the privilege to be able to work with all the lead actors from the first season again, but the freedom of the stories we're producing also allows to introduce brand new characters, new challenges, new genres and in some instances: new opportunity to push the boundaries and break new ground. After the first season premiered in July 2020, I listened very closely to the feedback, feelings and thoughts of our audience. From where we currently are in the pre-production phase at the time of writing, I am *beyond* excited to return to the set and see these stories come alive.

SPOTLIGHT | written by Nathaniel Farah and Gage Oxley

A tumultuous two months leaves child-star Sam Cooke cancelled and cast aside in the public eye. Desperate to regain his place in the spotlight, he ventures into celebrity reality tv show 'Surveillance State'.

STREETLIGHT | written by Jessica Redhead and Gage Oxley

A man dead in a hotel room leaves questions unanswered, but homicide detective Jackie Lambert is hot on the heels of seventeen-year-old escort Callum, who finds a connection with a new client.

LOWLIGHT | written by Michael Houghton and Gage Oxley

A game of cat and mouse: after falling victim to deep-fake videos, straight Adonis Mitch seeks revenge, plunging into the dark web. As the surrealism of the online world bleeds into the real, the hunt for depraved perpetrator Arron grows violent.

FIRELIGHT | written by Gage Oxley

A chance encounter on a train pulls Kane and Jacob back into the suffocating exploration of their enigmatic feelings. But things have changed - England has hosted the Euro 96, Diana is dead, and Kane has a boyfriend.

FLOODLIGHT | written by Gage Oxley

After turning up to Alexia's book signing, Adam is on the run. But, he quickly falls for another. Elizabeth: charming, cool, and completely unaware to Adam's advancing disturbed fantasies which are starting to become a reality.

SEARCHLIGHT | written by Harley Mathews and Gage Oxley

Following on from Series One's special Season Finale starring Bruce Herbelin-Earle, the final episode of Season Two will be kept under wraps as we attempt to push boundaries in a ground-breaking special.

WITH THANKS

There are so many people who without, we would not have been able to produce A Series of Light. Oxygen operates as a complete non-profit with no external funding. Below are a list of cast, crew and individuals who have offered locations, props, equipment or their advice in order for us to produce A Series of Light to the best of our ability.

Max Allwood
Adam Ayadi
Alex Bamford
Lily Burgess
Sian Carry
Tiarnan Meely Clark
Mika Colombick
James Coutsavlis
Samuel Curry
Katy Doran
Alice Duggan
Nathaniel Farah
Rachel Frost
Rhys Gannon
Devon George
Sarah Gidley
Julia Goodinson
Thomas J. Harkness
Charlie Harris
Callum Hart
Fin Henderson
Bruce Herbelin-Earle
Eleanor Hodson
Jacob Holdsworth
Andy Horry

Michael Houghton
Charlotte Hudson
Luke Hudson
Jamie Hutchison
Liv Johnson
Ole Madden
Alexandra Marlin
Harley Mathews
Debbie Maturi
Nadine Al-Baghdadi McChrystal
Rose McLaughlin
Dale Monie
Rochelle Naylor
Verdy Martin Oliver
Edward Oxley
Deborah Oxley
Jack Parr
Ash Patel
Charlie Philips
Summer Vasare Piscikiate
Nadhia Porcelli
Poppy Potts
Faizan Raza
Jessica Redhead
Harrison Reiblein
Dom Richmond
Dan Sheppard
Jack Simpson
Harvey Wane
Jake Watkins
Liam Watson
Rebecca Whittle
Lia Zawilska

Printed in Great Britain
by Amazon

81221117R00066